A Personal Possession

'This is a truly original work. The idea behind the plot is clever and very unusual and has the effect of immediately riveting the reader's attention ... It is a very accomplished piece of work.' **Ruth Rendell**

The plan grew out of a joke.

In a small seaside town in Northern California, three women were sitting in a Honda. The three women were friends, but casual ones. Zora Hirsch was the tallest, and a widow. Eileen Brande, also widowed, was slightly built and looked smaller than she was. Sally Robinson had been married and divorced three times and was fiercely optimistic.

They'd been talking about men. Zora said, 'I certainly don't want to marry anybody. I would just like a man to go places with. A weekend lover would be nice.'

The ladies were all in their forties.

Zora said, 'What we need is one man— reasonably attractive. We could share him.'

Sally suggested taking an ad.

So they did, and the responses—pathetic, boastful, demented—flooded in.

And two months later, Sally Robinson was found murdered . . .

JEANNE HART

A Personal Possession

COLLINS, 8 GRAFTON STREET, LONDON W1

William Collins Sons & Co. Ltd
London · Glasgow · Sydney · Auckland
Toronto · Johannesburg

First published in the UK 1989
© 1987 by Jeanne Hart

British Library Cataloguing in Publication Data

Hart, Jeanne
    A personal possession.—(Crime Club)
    I. Title
    813'.54[F]

ISBN 0 00 232247 1

Printed in Great Britain by
William Collins Sons & Co. Ltd, Glasgow

To Marion Hart, my mother,
and
To the two Jeans, Jean Evans without whom I would never
have started, and Jean Peterson, without whom I would
never have finished.

I would like to thank Edith Cooper, Lieutenant Jan Tepper, Jane Johnson, Edith Queller, Muriel Brouwer, Marilyn Wallace, Corinne Wipke, and my three children for their many kinds of advice, support, and help.

CHAPTER ONE

The plan grew out of a joke.

The Greek Festival, the event that each August put the cap to summer, was coming to a close. The day had been one of unrelenting heat, and those who had waited until evening to visit the fair had found that, despite the bay a few blocks to the south, it was still hot. Around the smoking souvlakia stand and the tables of diples and loukoumades and at the corner booth where beer and retsina were sold, damp bodies pressed and struggled for place. The irritable voices of children and crying babies mingled with the *Opa*'s of those who ringed the dancers,

1

and both were lost in bursts of bouzouki music. The noise made it seem hotter.

At the gate the three women fought their way past those still entering and paused outside.

Zora leaned against a parking meter and took a deep breath. "Remind me to skip this circus next year, will you?" She plucked her damp shirt from her ribs.

In their differences, the three made a striking group. Zora Hirsch, the tallest, was slender, with a tense, clever face and short dark hair touched at the temples with white. Her silk shirt and tailored slacks contrasted with the jeans, denim skirts and T-shirts coming and going through the festival gates and lent a formality to her figure. The small, gently rounded woman, Sally Robinson, was more casually dressed and wore on her mischievous face oversized horn-rimmed eyeglasses. The third of the group, Eileen Brande, was so slightly built that she seemed smaller than she was. Soft wings of hair, the copper lately muted by gray, framed her delicately modeled face, and about her hung an appealing air of uncertainty.

Zora straightened and poked a hand into her bag. "Damn. Why aren't my keys where they should be?"

"Try your pocket," suggested Eileen. "Where did we park? Down behind the library, wasn't it?"

They moved in that direction.

Sally was limping. "That lummox danced right over my foot, that good-looking one. I hope he didn't break anything." Indignation pulled her small round figure taut.

They turned into the tree-lined street. Above them, the full moon silvered the leaves of the eucalyptus and liquidambar.

"Oh, well," Sally said, "even if I never walk again, it's been quite a day." She laughed. "Peachy keen, you might say." Doggedly sanguine through three marriages and three divorces, Sally nurtured a fierce optimism. "You'll come back again next August, Zora. I always swear I won't, too, but August rolls around and I start thinking that this time I'll meet a dashing Greek with hard eyes and—"

Zora broke in with a delicate snort. "Tender hands?" She was rummaging in her handbag again. "Been reading Harlequins lately?" She grinned.

Sally's face grew warm. "Come on, Zora, you liked that one man."

Zora shrugged. "I liked him, but his hard eyes slid right past me. I never had a chance to check out the hands."

Sally glanced at her with doubt.

"They do get fat after a certain age, though, don't they—Greeks?" Eileen said. "Do you suppose they like any music besides bouzouki?"

"Some do and some don't. Like anybody," Zora said, her tone flat. Zora was a woman of firm principle.

The other two exchanged glances. "Watch it there, Eileen," Sally said.

"Here are my keys, right here." Zora pulled her hand from her pocket.

Eileen shook her head. "Two blocks back I said look in your pocket. The woman just doesn't listen."

Laughing, they piled into the Honda.

Zora fished her cigarettes from the glove compartment, lit one and started the motor. Sally settled herself in the back and removed one sandal with care. "You know," she said, "it isn't that it has to be a Greek with hard eyes or even a Greek at all. Or anybody in particular, really. I certainly don't ever again want to marry anybody. I would just like a man to go places with, some companionship. And maybe a little sex. A weekend lover would be nice."

Eileen sighed. "Me, too—that's exactly what I want." She opened her window and waved a hand in the direc-

3

tion of the smoke from Zora's cigarette. "At our age, who wants a husband? They wind up with midlife crises and heart attacks and you're worse off than before. But someone to go to concerts with . . ."

Zora laughed. "What we need is one man—reasonably attractive. We could share him. He could take you to concerts, me to films, Sally to the theater and folk dancing. Think of the rich cultural life he'd have."

"How about sex? Do you think one man could manage all of us?" The question did not emerge with quite the airiness Sally had intended.

"He might regard it as an intriguing challenge," said Zora.

She swung the car onto Cliff Drive. Below them under the bright moon the water softly breathed. Looking down on it, they grew quiet. In the silence of the car, it was as though each of them had sighed.

After a while Sally spoke, her voice wistful. "I get him Saturday nights," she said.

No one said anything for a moment; then Zora spoke. "We should run an ad. Seriously. Three women, early fifties . . ."

"Early fifties? Couldn't it be late forties?" Eileen protested.

"Right, why not? I've heard women always lie in those ads. Three women, late forties, seeking companionable man to act as escort—"

"And for sex," said Sally.

"And for stud purposes."

"Zora!"

"All right, Eileen, just being funny. For occasional friendly intimacy. What else should we ask for? How about hard eyes, for Sally?"

"Intelligent," said Eileen. "He has to be intelligent. And he has to like books and music—good music, symphonic and chamber." She played in the local symphony.

"How about jazz? If he's for me, he has to have a sense of humor," said Zora. "And be a movie buff, so he can take me to the Barnhouse every time they have a good film. I missed the new Bergman—they kept it just one week."

The Honda turned off the shore drive and began to climb the hill. Outside the open car windows the air was beginning to cool.

"What else? Would we want him younger?" Sally was two years older than the others.

"For the sex, you mean?" Zora caught her eye in the rearview mirror.

"I just thought . . ."

"Sally," Eileen said, "you need a separate man all for yourself. You can keep him tucked up in bed waiting for you."

Sally made sounds of protest.

Back at Eileen's, they opened a bottle of white zinfandel.

Eileen dumped a can of cocktail peanuts into a Waterford bowl. "You know," she said, her voice plaintive, "it really isn't fair. There are so many of us widows and divorcées and so few men, and then we can't do anything about it. Even if I had assertiveness training, I could never call a man for a date. Liberation came too late for me."

Sally nodded. "That's why we should really do the ad thing."

Eileen made a little sound of disgust. "Oh, Sally, what kind of weird characters would we attract if we advertised for one man for three women?"

"The ratio's about right," Zora remarked. She lay back in her chair, legs stretched before her, ankles crossed, rocking her wineglass and studying the amber liquid in the lamplight.

Elegant, Sally thought. But no matter how Zora af-

5

fected relaxation, the poised tension of her body belied her. Thinking of her own curved softness, Sally sighed. No one would ever call her elegant. But—and she was cheered by the reflection—neither would they describe her as tense.

Zora continued. "Think how efficient it would be—we could jointly screen applicants. Maybe we should do it just to see what kinds of kooks answer those ads."

"Wouldn't we be kooks, too?" Sally asked, grave.

"But we're not serious. And if by any chance we turn up someone interesting, so much the better for us and him. Let's do it for the hell of it."

"It sounds a little mean. To the men, if we're not serious," Sally said. "Besides, we couldn't use our real names and addresses. It would be too risky."

"That's true. We wouldn't want to turn up the Want Ad Killer. Or the Lonelyhearts Murderer. We could use one of our maiden names and take a post office box," Zora said.

"Or make up a name," said Sally.

"Doesn't the post office ask for ID's when you take a box?" asked Eileen.

"We could use a student mail service like that place over on Willow," Sally said. "I'm sure all they want is your money." She was warming to the idea.

Now that the ad was about to become a reality, Eileen became hesitant. "But what could we say in an ad? It's crazy."

Sally's answer was prompt. "If it were just mine, I'd say, 'Cuddly woman wants cuddly man with intelligence.'"

"Humor—we'd have to mention humor," Zora insisted. "What do they say in those damned ads? Let's look at one—you must have *Happy Times* here somewhere."

They studied the local entertainment tabloid.

6

"Why do these wonderful people have to advertise?" asked Sally. "They're all beautiful, young, open-minded—open-minded means something, doesn't it? Swapping or something kinky? None of them smoke, they love to hike and listen to music . . ."

"Music? Where? Which one?" Eileen bent over the open paper. "Oh, he's twenty-eight. Twenty-eight! Why would anybody twenty-eight have to advertise for a companion?"

By the time they had finished another glass of wine, the ad was written:

> *Three women, late forties, attractive, educated, who enjoy talk, music, books, theater, folk danc- ing, films, would enjoy meeting one man to keep them (one at a time) company. Must be intel- ligent, have a sense of humor, be warm, relaxed. We are not looking for sex, group or otherwise, but for interesting companionship.*

"A man like this doesn't exist," said Eileen.

"He might. It's a good ad," said Zora. "We might meet someone interesting. And if something happens beyond companionship, it happens. We're not asking for it."

The other two stared at her. "Well," said Sally. "You!"

Zora looked offended. "I'm not above it all, you know. This crusty exterior hides a . . . vulnerable heart."

"No," said Eileen, "but you always sound so . . . so . . ."

"So . . . what?" Sally and Zora chorused. Eileen's un- finished sentences were an irritant to her friends. "Finish it, Eileen," said Sally.

"Down-to-earth. Common sense. Cool."

"Cool?" Zora grinned. "It's all a fake. I'm sure I'd be a pushover for the right man; I just find it harder than most

7

to locate him." She put out her cigarette and refrained from reaching for another. "What about a name for the post box? We can't have three names on it."

"I'll tell you what," said Sally. "I'll let you have the pick of my husbands' names. I'd even throw in the husbands if I still had them." Sally treated her past with a grand carelessness.

"All but Robinson," said Zora.

"Robinson isn't a husband's name, it's mine—I took it back. My last husband's name, I'll have you know, was James Freeman Carr the Third. More name than man, Jim was."

Zora stood abruptly and crossed the room to refill her glass.

Sally turned to her. "I know. I shouldn't say things like that. I just don't feel generous when it comes to Jim. It's not like you—I wasn't widowed, I chose to leave." She sighed. "He was all right, I guess. But *we* weren't all right."

Zora returned to her chair without comment.

"Let's hear the rest about your husbands," Eileen said. "Don't mind Zora—you have to say what you think."

Sally nodded. "I know. Where was I?"

"Who was the first one?" asked Eileen.

"The first one—in some ways, he was really the best, but we were just too young—was Tip Creatore. Almost five years that one lasted; I married him when I was eighteen. After our divorce, I took a job in Chicago and there I met Roger. Roger Ashe. We were married for twenty-one years—he's Nicky's father. He's still there in our old town house. Then"—she puffed out her cheeks and raised her brows—"when I was forty-four—" She stopped. "Do you really want to know all this?"

"I've always wondered about it," said Eileen. "But if you . . ."

"I don't mind. I like to talk about myself. Well, when I

was forty-four, I was swept off my feet. I suppose I was having a case of last-chance-itis or something, but I really thought Jim was *it*. It lasted four years—then I left him."

"Only four years? And you—" Eileen began.

"I know. Afterwards I was sorry about the whole thing. Roger was such a nice, comfortable man, and I was so used to him. And Nicky was torn apart by our divorce. It was a mess—unnecessary, crazy. It was like coming down with something. Except that when my head cleared, I discovered how much damage I'd done."

Eileen leaned toward her. "What do you mean?"

"Oh, Nicky was just at that funny uncertain age. He didn't know what he was all about, and there I was, in essence saying his father was no good, that I didn't want him. And Jim never understood or helped—what did he know about kids? I don't think Nicky's ever forgiven me."

"Really, Sally," said Zora, her voice crisp. "When I met Nicky at your Christmas party, he was being perfectly pleasant to you."

"That's not it, it's—he's never really had a girl. I think that's because of me. I don't mean he's gay—he just doesn't seem too good at relationships. Any kind."

"How did your—Jim take your leaving him?" asked Zora.

"Not well. He's a self-important man, really a vain, weak man in most ways." She paused. "He is, Zora, he really is—I'm not just being spiteful. And it's funny, I knew that, I always knew it, but somehow he could charm me every time."

"I don't see how, if you saw him that way," Eileen said.

"He was wonderful-looking, that was part of it. I think I was flattered at having someone so handsome want me. Anyway, finally I decided I'd had it. I think he was bored by then, too, but of course he claimed he

9

couldn't live without me. The problem for him was that after years of being a bachelor, he had finally married. He'd given his precious self to me in marriage, and then I'd been the one to leave. That was hard for him to take."

For a moment no one spoke. Then Eileen said, "I understand."

The other two turned to her.

She flushed. "I mean about bad marriages. I've never told anyone this, but my marriage was miserable."

"But I thought—" Sally said.

"I know. I never talk about it. My husband was a cold man, self-centered." She shivered. "I suppose he wasn't different from lots of men."

"What do you mean?"

"He never had time for us, for me and our sons. You hear it over and over from your friends—why is he always working, why doesn't he talk to me? The terrible thing is that he was attractive; other people probably thought I was lucky."

Sally nodded. "But you didn't think so. He sounds like the standard workaholic."

"It wasn't just work. Oh, he was interested in his cello, but—no, that's not even true, all he was interested in was his concert reviews. He was like a spoiled"—she shook her head, at a loss for the precise word—"pop star, maybe, for all he cared about the music."

"How on earth did he become a concert cellist?" Zora asked.

"He'd studied as a kid and his teacher thought he was Janos Starker." She paused to consider. "You know, I'm not being fair. He did love the music, I'm sure, but he was more in love with the idea of himself, Ernest Brande, concert cellist, than with any other thing."

"But, Eileen," Sally said, "you love music. I'd have thought it'd have brought you together."

Eileen laughed. "It did. It was ironic, really—we met

in music school. I thought the music would be a marvelous thing we'd share. Instead—"

"Yes?" Sally said.

"Instead he was away all the time, and when he was home—well, I used to long, absolutely long, for him to talk to me about what he was doing, what I was doing, about the two boys—anything."

"And he didn't."

"Right, Zora. All he wanted was that I be there in his bed when he came back to town. . . . You know, sometimes when he was home"—her voice crackled with anger—"I would lie and hate him while we . . . you couldn't call what we did making love. I'd never known I could be so full of hate." Then, as though she had glimpsed her own hot face, she stopped. "I'm sorry. I don't know what . . . I guess I've just never gotten over it." She pushed her hair back from her forehead in an exhausted little gesture. "Before I overflowed with all this, what were we saying?"

"The ad. The name for the ad," Sally said.

"Maybe," said Zora, "we should forget about the ad. It seems to have produced a lot of emotion." She reached to pat Eileen's shoulder in an awkward little gesture.

"No," said Eileen, "let's go ahead. I'm sorry I . . . What name shall we use? Sally, you said your first husband was named—?"

"Creatore."

"Yes. Let's use that."

"Fine with me." Sally stood up, tiredness washing over her. "I should go."

Zora reached for her bag. "Me, too. Let's use Teresa for a first name. How's that?"

Eileen nodded. "I'll be over on Willow tomorrow. I can get the box and mail the ad."

Zora laid an arm across Eileen's shoulders. "Don't worry about what you said."

11

"No." Sally turned to hug Eileen. "I'm glad you told us. Talking helps."

"I know." Eileen ran her hand over her face. "I just . . . It just isn't like me to . . ."

"Forget it," said Sally, giving her another squeeze. She pulled on her quilted jacket. No matter how hot the day, the evenings were cool. "You're the only one, Zora," she said. "You seem to have had all the luck."

"Luck?" Zora laughed shortly. "I wouldn't put it quite like that. What about loss? What about what you feel when you have had a good relationship—loved someone completely—and then you lose him? Maybe you're the lucky ones."

"You're right," said Eileen. "There's never anything lucky about being a widow, not anything."

Outside the air was fresh, a little chilly. The three stood in the open door, saying nothing.

After a while, Sally spoke. "Three sad middle-aged ladies. And lonely." She sighed. "Here's to our big adventure," she said.

No one smiled.

CHAPTER TWO

The number of answers to the ad surprised them.

They had agreed to wait a full two weeks after the Greek Festival and then to meet at Eileen's to see what the response had been.

After her husband's death, Eileen had stayed on in the house that was too large for one person. She needed room for her sons to visit, she told herself, but in fact the decision had come out of inertia. To move the Steinway, to find in this California seaside town another setting for the formal gray-patterned sofa, the velvet chairs, the or-

13

molu clock, the Chinese cabinets, all the controlled rhythms of her life, seemed a task beyond her energies. It had simply been easier to stay in the place that had become home after she and her husband had turned their backs on Chicago.

Zora and Sally arrived at Eileen's at the same moment.

"Wait till you see," Eileen greeted them. Over her dining table, obliterating its polished surface, lay the answers to their advertisement.

"My," said Sally. "We must be good." The melancholy was gone, she had suppressed her anxieties about Nicky, regained her cheerful perspective and, she announced, lost two pounds.

"Most of them are awful," Eileen said. "They don't even pretend to be interested in anything but sex. Look at this, for example."

They bent over the table:

> Dear Box 4609,
>   Listen, we both know what your after. Let's cut the crap and just do it. I'll meet you when you say.
>
>   K. Jensen

"Here's another. There were a lot like that."

> Whoever you are, I think I'm the guy for you. My girlfriends tell me they thought they were frigid before they met me. Now they can't get enough of it. Just say when. Always ready. Call me at the number below.
>
>   Big Bob

"And then there's this kind," Eileen went on.

> Dear Seekers After Experience:
>   There are sexual horizons toward which you

14

may not have looked. If you have never tried
group sex in all its permutations, you have barely
seen the tip of the iceberg . . .

"He goes on, merrily mixing metaphors and detailing the marvels we haven't, thank God, experienced. The letter was so weird it made me feel a little sick."

But some of the letters were sad. One especially stopped them:

> *I have been alone since my wife died. I never talk*
> *to nobody. Just sit in my room or walk around on*
> *the streets. I would like somebody sometime to*
> *make me dinner and then just sit and be quiet to-*
> *gether. I don't want nothing physical. Please*
> *write.*

"That's pitiful," Sally said. "Can't you just see that poor little man walking around downtown on the mall all by himself? It makes me want to cry."

"But not want to write him," said Zora. "Unless we refer him to Family Service or someplace."

"I think we should do that," said Sally.

"If we don't write something to him, he'll haunt me," said Eileen. "But wait. There are a couple of good ones— three, actually."

Sally brightened. "One for each of us?"

"I'm not so sure," said Eileen. "I don't know if I really want to go through with this. Some of these letters are pathetic and some are just dumb, but some of them are so strange, I'm not sure I want to take a chance on meeting any of these people."

Gravely, they read the three letters.

"Don't you think this one's best?" asked Eileen. "If we try anyone, I'm for trying him."

15

Once more they read his letter:

> *Ladies:*
> *This could be the answer to every man's dream—three women at once. I'm 55, quite adequately educated, I go to concerts willingly and enjoy films. Of course I read. I think I would be described as intelligent. I have a sense of humor or I would not be answering this ad. Would one or all of you care to meet me? How about a coffee house? My phone number (after 6 p.m.) is below.*
>
> *Paul Shapiro*

"He sounds nice," said Sally with some doubt. "Do you think it's risky?"

"It needn't be," said Zora. "Look, we've screened out the impossibles. All they know is Teresa Creatore." She paused. "No, they don't even know that, do they—only we and the post office know." She laughed. "I love that name. In my next incarnation, I'm going to be Teresa Creatore. I think I'll be a diva. Another Julia Migenes-Johnson." She returned to the letters. "We've already decided we'll meet whomever we meet at the Kettle House, haven't we—the outdoor cafe? This man seems to be thinking right along the same lines. We can set things up so the other two are right there at the next table, within earshot. We'll play it cool and give out no addresses or last names. We can't have an adventure if we don't do anything."

"How'll we pick?" asked Eileen. "Didn't we say we'd have one person at a time meet him?"

"Draw lots. Or volunteer. Really, what we ought to do is make it the one of us most likely to interest him, so he'll want to go on," said Zora. She closed her eyes in thought. "What did your high school yearbooks say about you two?"

Sally stared. "*High* school?"

"Mine said, 'See you at Carnegie Hall,'" said Eileen. "So much for predictions."

"Would you believe," Sally told them, "mine said, 'Sweetheart of the Senior Class.' That was my popular year."

"There you are. Made to order. Mine must have been spectacular, I can't even remember it. I think Sally should go first, but I will, Sal, if you're nervous."

"I'm not—very. Unless you want to, Eileen."

"Not me. I'll wait till we've looked him over. You'll have to phone him tonight."

"He must work," said Zora.

"Of course he works. He's only fifty-five," said Sally. She paused. "He'll think I'm in my forties."

"Not if he's smart," said Zora.

Sally threw her an angry glance. "Thanks a lot."

"Jesus, you're touchy. I just mean he'll assume you've knocked off a few years. Maybe he has."

They contemplated the thought.

"Nothing to do but try," said Zora. "If he's decrepit or awful, that's that. But remember, Sally, only first names."

Sally nodded. "Only first names. We'll protect ourselves."

Kettle House was made up of an indoor restaurant and an outdoor cafe and was located on the town's mall, so called, a one-lane street lined with trees and dotted with brick containers filled with marigolds, nemesias and petunias. The cafe was separated from the public by a low hedge. At noon a jazz combo performed, and the area beyond the hedge was populated by interested street peo-

17

ple perched on the rims of the mall's raised flower beds and by passersby strolling more slowly than necessary.

Kettle House opened at eleven-thirty. Until noon most of the tables were empty; Sally and Paul Shapiro had agreed to meet just before noon.

Sally arrived early. Shortly after, the other two women entered and seated themselves at a nearby table.

Paul had described himself; Sally had said she would wear a red dress.

"Red?" Eileen had said. "Doesn't that seem a little. . . ?"

"He has to find me," Sally countered with irritation. "It's the only distinctive garment I own. You really are such a puritan, Eileen."

Precisely at twelve he arrived. They spotted him before his eyes settled on the brick-colored linen of Sally's dress and he headed toward her. He was, just as he had told her, a stocky man of medium height with whitening hair and a deep tan. "Sally?" he said.

Her face grew warm. "Yes . . . Paul?" At the other table the two women, with elaborate unconcern, pointed out to each other items on the menu. "Sit down. I feel a little silly."

He grinned. "It's a silly situation. I've always wanted to answer one of those ads. I've read them for years. Well. How about some wine and a little lunch?"

"Yes. You needn't pay for it, you know, we're just here to—"

He laughed. "How much do you plan to eat?"

After they had ordered wine, he sat back, looking at her. "Now how did all this come about? How did you happen to run an ad like that?"

"It was really a joke, to begin with."

"I thought so. I could just imagine you and your friends having some sort of conversation and then saying, 'Why not?'"

18

"We did. That's exactly what happened."

"And you were nervous about it."

"I still am." She looked at him uncertainly. "You aren't married?"

He tipped his head back and laughed. "You'd better worry about more than the man's being married, if you're going to make a habit of this sort of thing. No, I'm not married. I was—just so you'll know there's nothing strange about me. I was married for twenty-five years, but at present I am all legally divorced and free of encumbrance. And you, I gather, are not married."

"No. Divorced, too." She studied his face. "Did you. . . ? Twenty-five years is a long time."

"It is. I was quite willing for it to be longer. I was not suffering from male menopause or whatever the syndrome is called. My wife, unfortunately, became liberated from such things as marriage. Not," he added, "that I want to give the impression that I'm anti-feminist. My wife just went a bit overboard. The waves she made swept me right out of her life." He looked away.

"You sound sad."

"The first ten years of our marriage we lived in a fourth-floor walk-up. Every night after work, I ran up the stairs." He smiled faintly. "However, what about you?"

"I guess I *was* having a mid-life crisis. Twenty-one years down the drain. Let's not talk about it."

"Let's not. You're not working, I gather?"

"Oh, I am. Part time, at the university. I used to be an executive secretary—now they call them administrative assistants. Sounds better, same work. You?"

"Marine biology. Richards Labs. I expect to work till I die. What else would I do with myself?"

"You could escort ladies." She laughed. "I guess that wouldn't take full time."

"With three it might." He regarded her solemnly.

19

"Aren't you afraid, meeting men you know nothing about? I could be a serial murderer, for all you know."

The waitress, arriving to take their lunch order, caught his last sentence and looked at him with interest.

As she moved away, Sally said, "I know. We did think of it. But we figured people answer those ads all the time. The papers are full of them. Are you a serial murderer?"

"Of course. Why else would I mention it?"

Over the wineglasses they sat looking at each other with mutual appreciation.

"Tell me about you," he said.

"Well, what? I had a happy childhood. I've spent my life getting over a happy childhood. I was born in Cedar Rapids—a solid family. Solid." She laughed. "My father was a high school principal with an absolutely irreproachable reputation, not that I realized it then. My mother had taught elementary school. And I, I was the youngest of three. I had two brothers who alternately doted on me and tormented me. I think the thing that saved me was that my parents went in for a sort of benign neglect."

"It sounds like the kind of childhood all of us would have liked to get over."

"And you?"

"Entirely different. New York. Second generation." He grinned. "That means immigrant parents. Public schools and City College. My parents loved me and wanted to see me started, educated, but once they gave up the hope of my being a doctor, they left me alone to develop along my own lines. Can't fault parents like that."

"And you have kids?"

"Yes, three grown ones. A daughter, two sons. They aren't any of them going to be doctors, either." He grinned.

"But you don't care."

"No. All I hoped for was that they'd get through school without becoming drug addicts. They managed to succeed there. They're good kids. I don't see a lot of them."

"I see mine, but he worries me. But that's another story. So"—she found she was unable to meet his eyes—"you like the idea of being shared by three women?" The notion was now less appealing to her than it had been the evening of the Greek Festival.

"I don't know whether or not I like it. All men have fantasies and I'm no different, but my fantasies aren't precisely what you ladies had in mind."

Sally's face was grave. "I'm not really sure what we did have in mind. To me, it didn't seem quite real. When we ran the ad, I mean. Am I making any sense?"

"Not much. But do you now find it real?" He studied her face.

"Oh, yes. It's real, all right." She found herself squirming under his level stare. "You're very real." Her eyes met his. "Very."

Afterwards the three women met at Zora's.

Settled in the living room, Sally sighed. "I do love this house." She stroked the pale linen of the sofa. "Your *rugs*. I've never been intimately associated with beautiful rugs before."

"I know where you can buy some." Rugs were Zora's business as well as her passion. Her shop, Rug Repertoire, had become so popular that by now she was able to restrict her own participation to buying trips.

"Ha," said Sally. "Not on *my* income, I can't." She looked around.

Zora had gutted the Victorian house, then stripped and sanded it till it was a bare, clean backdrop for her rugs. Everywhere their glowing colors and subtle textures caught the eye—the tarnished crimson of a Bokhara, the

21

neat flat weave of a Khilim, a Soumak, a Merghoum—
little explosions of color against the stark setting.

"I'm even getting so I know some of their names,"
Eileen said, indicating the mosaic pattern of one. "That's
a Shirvan. I think. Is it?"

Zora nodded. "It is. Now. About Paul."

Lovely. He was a lovely man, they agreed, every bit as
delightful as his letter.

"The man we thought didn't exist," said Eileen.

"Maybe. Anyway, a real find," agreed Sally, as though
she had just uncovered a designer model on a sales rack.
"Of course, he doesn't folk dance."

Zora was thoughtful. "So charming he's a little . . .
fishy?"

"I trusted him," said Sally.

"Me, too. I liked him," said Eileen. "And I was the
most suspicious at first. I'll even go next to meet him."

"I hate to share him," said Sally.

Eileen was indignant. "We agreed beforehand—"

"I don't mean it," Sally broke in. "Wouldn't it be
awful, though, if one of us fell in love with him? Awful
for the others, I mean?"

"It would depend," said Zora, "on whether or not he
fell in love, too. I can think of a number of awful pos-
sibilities."

None of the three wished to discuss them. The next
meeting, it was decided, was to be between Eileen and
Paul.

"It's fine with me," said Zora. "He isn't my type at all,
though he'll do just fine for escort purposes."

"What's wrong with him?" asked Sally.

"Escort purposes was all we had in mind," said Eileen
tartly.

"Nothing's wrong with him, he's just—well, I like big
men, gentle ones, not that small, intense, energetic sort. I

like to be the one with the energy." She reached for her cigarettes.

"He's not small," protested Sally and Eileen in a voice.

"He looked a lot taller than I, and I'm five six," said Eileen. "Anybody's taller than Sally."

Sally, offended, threw an annoyed glance her way.

"One thing, though," said Eileen, "I know I'll never be able to talk to him with both of you breathing down our necks. I'm too . . . shy, I guess. Now that we've all seen him, looked him over, let me go by myself. I'll meet him someplace safe, even Kettle House again."

Sally regarded her with suspicion. "I had to have people listening over my shoulder. I'm shy, too."

The other two laughed.

"Well, I am. Are you sure that's why you want to be alone with him?"

Eileen was sure. "You don't know what shy means," she said. "I'm not so bad now, but back in high school. . .! My classmates used to blurt out personal things to just anyone and talk to teachers about their private affairs. I couldn't even raise my voice without blushing. Even now, sometimes . . ."

This was one of those days.

Shyness engulfed her as she waited at a table, a different table from the one she had shared with Zora earlier. What they were doing suddenly seemed ludicrous, filled with threat, impossible. How had a sober, intelligent woman like herself, comfortable only with people she knew well, become involved in this exploit? She could feel one of her headaches beginning.

She had just risen from her seat to leave when Paul Shapiro appeared.

Her identification of herself had been less vivid than Sally's. He sounded unsure. "Eileen? Mauve silk shirt?"

She sat down again. "Paul?" Her voice sounded small to her.

"I realized after we spoke that I wasn't sure what color mauve is. In novels, mauve and taupe and puce have always confused me. Pink—or is it purple?"

Eileen looked down at her shirt. "I could just have said pink."

He sat down. "Do you folk dance, too?"

She laughed, suddenly more comfortable. "No. Music is my . . . thing."

"What kind of music?"

"All kinds. I play the violin."

"But that's wonderful."

"Wonderful?"

"When I was a boy I took violin lessons. It was a thing Jewish boys in a certain New York stratum did. Secretly I loved the idea, but I was adamant in my refusal to learn. My punishment was Hebrew school." He smiled. "Don't look for the logic in it. My parents weren't enthusiastic about bar mitzvahs, but they seemed to feel I must give evidence of knowing something. So I became a man, officially. They never troubled me with religion—or the violin—again." He looked around. "The other two aren't here?"

Eileen flushed. "Should they be?"

"They were last time. That is, you were, with someone else. I noticed—that's why I was pretty sure it was you today. Were you checking me out, or protecting Sally?"

"Both, I guess. This is a pretty crazy idea."

"Dangerous, I'd say. On the other hand, if it hadn't been such a crazy ad, I wouldn't have answered it." He looked at her. "That would have been too bad."

The second conference was less happy.

They met in the park outside the library. Above them

the blossoms of the red-flowering gum stirred. Beyond its branches the sky was cloudless, a cobalt backdrop.

Sally's mood did not reflect the serenity of the day. "You certainly took your time."

"I don't want to go on with this," said Eileen.

"Why?" Sally pulled back her shoulders, as she did when she was angry. "You're cheating Zora out of her turn."

"Zora can do what she wants. It's a lunatic idea and I don't know how I got involved in it. You can both do what you want. Just leave me out."

"Didn't you like him? Were you afraid or something?" Sally insisted.

"Wait," said Zora. "Maybe she's right. We don't know one thing about him except that you found him charming, Sally. Some of the world's most famous sociopaths are charming."

"I'm not afraid of him." Eileen was irritable. "It's just crazy, three women and one man. He's a person, not some sort of . . . robot escort. We're bound to have feelings about him, and *then* what do we do? And what does *he* do?"

"Don't you want your turn, Zora?" Sally said.

Zora laughed. "We sound like a bunch of four-year-olds in nursery school. No, I don't care—really. I'm curious, but it looks as though we may be in enough trouble with just the two of you meeting him. Maybe this wasn't such a good idea."

"You go once at least," Sally said, stubborn. "Maybe talk to him about what *he* thinks about the whole idea. You're good at organizing things. You'll know what to do."

"She doesn't have to ask him. I talked to him about what he thinks of the idea," said Eileen. "Among other things, he thinks it's dangerous."

"He didn't tell you he was dangerous, did he?"

"Of course not. But he said we just didn't know what sort of person we might meet that way—it could be anybody. We talked about it for quite a while."

"But the fact is," said Zora, "we're three perfectly ordinary women, and he seems to be an ordinary man. Maybe we were just lucky. It's the sharing business that appears to be the problem." She looked at the other two with amusement. "You both liked him, didn't you?"

"Don't be so superior, Zora." Eileen's voice was sharp.

"Anyway," said Sally, "whether or not we all see him, I still want to."

"No," said Eileen. "That wouldn't be fair."

"Why not? You want out. You said to do as we wish."

"It just isn't what we agreed. You go advertise for your cuddly man."

"This man seems perfectly cuddly to me." Sally's laugh was not pleasant.

Eileen stood up so suddenly her bag fell from her lap. "Do what you please. I'm going."

"Wait," Zora said. "Don't go away mad. This was just an experiment—an adventure. For God's sake, don't let's turn it into a battlefield."

"I'm not angry," Eileen said in a tight voice. "I have things to do." She looked at her wristwatch. "I'm late as it is."

"Well." Sally poked in her handbag for the paper on which she had written Paul's phone number, twisted it into a knot and sailed it into the litter basket. "I guess that's the end of Paul. So much for good ideas." She sounded cross.

"If it *was* a good idea," said Zora. "You go along. I have to stop at the shop."

After they had gone, she continued to sit on the bench. Finally she sighed and rose. "Shit," she said aloud. "We should have known better."

The man on the next bench glanced at her, startled, and then quickly looked away.

CHAPTER THREE

The body was discovered by the cleaning woman; she came on Mondays and had her own keys. On that October morning, she had let herself in promptly at nine.

Detective Carl Pedersen read the newspaper account in his office between mouthfuls of the cheeseburger he had picked up for dinner. This was his fifth dinner in the office and—what, ninth?—away from home. Freda's casseroles, thoughtfully stored in the freezer before she had left to help Carey with the new baby, remained untouched. He wondered if in time, when he had grown

27

weary enough of pizzas and hamburgers, he would remember about defrosting. Probably Freda would be back before then.

He pried the cap off the milkshake, licked its underside and folded his newspaper to the item. He was always curious to see what the press would do with the facts they had been given—and *to* the facts.

They had made the most of what they had, placing the story on the first page beneath a modest caption. Tomorrow would probably bring photographs, expanded details. Time was when a murder in this town would have been a major piece of news, featured beneath a screaming banner. Not now.

LOCAL WOMAN FOUND DEAD

Police today were looking for clues in the death of the fifty-three-year-old university employee and amateur actress Sally Robinson, who was found beaten in her Lincoln Street home this morning.

The victim, former wife of the internationally known art collector James Freeman Carr III, was employed part time in the university's admissions office but was best known locally for her character roles with The Players, Bay Cove's civic theater group.

The discovery was made by Mrs. Tamiko Nishikawa, of Albert Street, who told Patrol Officer Edward Kuneo of the Bay Cove Police, "I went in the way I always do, using my two keys. I noticed a lamp had been left on in the living room. I went in to turn it off and saw her lying in front of the fireplace. I could see she was dead."

Investigators said they had not determined a motive for the slaying. Detective Carl Pedersen said there were no signs of forced entry or burglary.

Robinson is survived by a son from a previous marriage, Nicholas Ashe, 20.

Newsmen interested Pedersen; their persistence and re-sourcefulness struck a sympathetic chord in him, but he considered them unpredictable. This time the *Bay Cove Banner* had not done badly. He glanced at the story again. Character parts. He had been trying to place her, but he could not recall, unless . . . the mother in that last play, the small jaunty woman gesturing with plump hands? Freda, who saw that they never missed a play, would know. He glanced at the clock. The Berkeley Police had finally located the son.

Earlier Pedersen had spoken with the neighbors and with Mrs. Nishikawa, small, neat-featured, with sharp, frightened eyes. Pedersen's wife was small and dark-haired, but Mrs. Nishikawa was smaller, her hair a glossy black helmet.

He had to listen closely although Mrs. Nishikawa was proud of her English. She had attended night classes for the foreign-born. "Six year, I go." She giggled. "Every Wednesday. My husband get mad." She had married in the United States, a Nisei. She didn't have to work; she did it, she explained, so she and her girlfriends could go once a month to Reno. Here she giggled again. "Fifty dollar I take," she said, her eyes mischievous. "No more. Over year, break even." She was from Hiroshima, she told him without emotion.

Mrs. Nishikawa's knowledge of Sally Robinson was more extensive than her employer might have guessed, but Pedersen sensed that she was feeding him information with caution. Yes, Miss Robinson had many friends—two were women she called Zora, funny name, and Eileen; Miss Robinson often talked on the phone with one or the other. The Robinson address book, which now lay on his desk, had given their full names: Zora Hirsch and Eileen Brande. Miss Robinson was also fond of several people in her theater group: Lou, Simone, and a person

29

she called Mullen. "Maybe last name?" said Mrs. Nishikawa.

Yes, she did go out with men, but Mrs. Nishikawa knew no names. On one occasion she had seen a white-haired man with a young face—very nice, she thought him. A laughing face, she told Pedersen, tipping her own smooth little countenance toward him. She did not know the man's name. It amused Pedersen that he found her soothing. Talking with her made everything seem simple, merely a matter of time and his admirably precise investigation. He smiled.

Simple, of course, it was not. Sally Robinson's address book was solid with names.

Mrs. Nishikawa had not known Sally's son. She had helped once at a Christmas party and, as she had stood in the kitchen arranging shrimp around a bowl of dip, had heard him talking with his mother. But once in the dining room, she could not sort him out from the young people who had been invited from the theater. All she recalled of the conversation was that he sounded "funny—little mad" and told his mother not to nag any more about that. About what she did not know—or would not say.

When finally he rose to dismiss her, Pedersen saw that Mrs. Nishikawa was not as cool as she seemed. Her round little face was strained and, although it was clear she preferred not to reveal her emotion, she was trembling. He reached toward her and patted her hand.

She nodded at him ruefully. "Nice lady," she said. *"Nice."*

The next-door neighbors were less helpful than Mrs. Nishikawa. Neither had noticed anything out of the ordinary—no suspicious-looking cars, no strangers. Sally Robinson came and went, stopping to say hello if one of them was outdoors pulling a weed or picking up the

30

mail. She had gone beyond an easy front-yard exchange with only one person on the street.

Pedersen, whose wife exchanged anecdotes and Christmas fruitcake with the occupants of almost every house on his block and who himself had served numbers of them cold beer and charred frankfurters over his backyard barbecue, shook his head at the detachment of these people. What did it take today to make someone pay attention?

The one neighbor who had come to know Sally Robinson was a young mother three houses down, Belinda Larson. Her toddler had tumbled off his tricycle and cut his chin and, weeping herself, she had carried the sobbing child down the street and knocked on Sally Robinson's door. Sally had driven them to the hospital. After that they had visited back and forth. "Oh, she was great— Sally was a great person," the young woman assured him.

Belinda Larson looked more like someone's teenage sister than a mother. Small and thin, face clean of makeup, she had pulled her fair hair back with a childish barrette and was dressed in bleach-streaked jeans and a T-shirt which had ARMS ARE FOR HUGGING spelled across it in red.

"Sally loved Billy," she explained. "She kept saying she didn't think she'd ever be a grandmother, her son didn't have a girl or anything. But he's pretty young—I told her he had lots of time. I didn't have a baby till I was twenty-five. I'm almost thirty now." She frowned. "I don't *feel* that old," she added, as though surely there had been a mistake.

Pedersen grinned. "I know. I don't feel thirty, either."

She giggled, Sally forgotten for a moment.

"Did Miss Robinson have any particular man—boyfriend that you know of?"

31

She shook her head. "We never talked about things like that, we talked about"—she paused and looked surprised—"me and my family. I guess that was pretty selfish."

"It probably gave her a lot of satisfaction. Like having a daughter-in-law with a child."

She nodded. The corners of her mouth pulled down. "But who could have done that to her? We haven't had any break-ins in the neighborhood. And, you know, I remember her telling me that when she first bought the house she had deadbolts added. She thought it was silly, but her son made her do it."

"She may have opened the door to her murderer. Or brought him home."

"You mean, like . . . picked somebody up?"

"Perhaps you can tell me that. Do you know whether she went to bars—singles bars, for instance?"

"Oh, I don't think so, do you?"

"How about men in general? Did she see anyone—date?"

Belinda squinted in thought. "Gee, I'm sorry. I just don't remember her saying anything. I know I never saw anybody. Even this weekend. I'm not much help."

Pedersen smiled. "Can't tell me what you don't know. Was she worried about anything?"

"You mean like—oh, she was worried a little, about her age. She was fifty-three and she thought she looked older since she had . . . since the"—her face became pink—"menopause," she finished quickly. "I thought she looked pretty good for such—for somebody her age."

The door burst open and Billy invaded the room like a dive bomber. As she turned her attention to setting out a snack for her son, she added a final comment. "Her son, the one I told you about, was coming down this weekend."

Pedersen set his coffee cup down. "You saw him?"

"No, no. She just said he was coming and that it was a month since he'd been here. She was going to do some baking for him, a coffee cake she used to make when he was little."

"Did you see his car—or any strange car—over the weekend?"

"No, like I told you, there was nothing special. Nothing suspicious, I mean. Besides, Tom and I took Billy to the Exploratorium—you know, in San Francisco?—and we were away all day Sunday. Billy's pretty little for it, but we love it. So, really, we weren't here to see anything."

He stood up. "One last question and I'll let you get back to your son. Do you know whether or not Miss Robinson saw her former husband—the father of her son?"

"I don't think so. She told me he got married again. You knew she did, too?"

"Did she see *that* husband?"

"I don't know. She said he was here in the country— he lives in Europe someplace, you know. She said he called her one night. She seemed sort of surprised."

"When was this?"

"Oh, a week or so ago."

"Did she say anything about seeing him—or where he called from?"

"No. Or if she did, I can't remember. She said they had quite a talk. I was kind of curious, but she didn't say any more, and I think people have to have their privacy. If they don't tell me, I don't ask."

"A good practice." He smiled. "A little hard on me in a situation like this, but situations like this don't happen often."

"I hope not," she said fiercely.

Pedersen had just put his mouth around a bite of his second cheeseburger and felt the juices spurt against his pal-

33

ate when the young man for whom he had been waiting arrived. With regret, he replaced the rest of his meal on the paper plate and folded his napkin over it.

Then he looked at the boy and forgot the sandwich. My God, he thought, did he drive that winding mountain road like *that*? Nicholas Ashe's face was blanched and rigid with shock, his eyes glazed, unfocused.

"Here." Pedersen jerked a chair around. "Sit. Let me get you a cup of coffee."

The young man folded into the chair like someone toppling from a height. "Where is she?" His eyes darted around the room as though his mother were concealed somewhere in the office.

"Take time to pull yourself together. Did you drive down alone?"

"What? Oh . . . alone. Yes, I . . ." He turned a blank face toward Pedersen. He seemed to have forgotten what he had been asked.

"Drink your coffee." The image of his Matthew passed through his mind. "Take it easy, son," he murmured. "We have time. Sit a minute."

The young man swallowed his coffee in great nervous gulps, jerking the cup and spilling some of the dark liquid onto his gray trouser leg. He was tall, six two or three, with a well-muscled body, yet there was about him the look of a half-grown boy—the softness, the vulnerability and unformed aspect of a twelve-year-old who had not yet shaved. His features were regular enough; the oddness about his face, Pedersen decided, was not disproportion but some mirroring of his inner state. In part it was merely that he looked so stricken. Even his suntan, like jaundice over his bloodless face, offered no concealment, and his uneasy eyes, which had begun to come to life, moved as though unable to find a place to rest.

For a few minutes neither said anything. Then Pedersen spoke. "Steadier? Shall we see your mother now?"

34

The morgue was hidden away in the basement of the county hospital on the other side of town.

Some things about his job he hated.

Back in Pedersen's office, Nicholas Ashe sank into his chair and fixed his eyes on the floor. "They didn't . . . it wasn't as bad as I"—he drew a ragged breath—"as I was afraid it would be. To see her."

"No." Pedersen hesitated. "She was struck just the once." It had been a hard blow, though, and from behind. In her living room the brass fetish figure had been an innocent art object, an ornament; in the hands of the killer, it had been a lethal weapon.

The boy winced and looked away. "I was afraid . . . I wasn't sure. . . ."

"I know." The silence grew thick. Pedersen broke it. "They had a lot of trouble finding you. Where have you been all day?"

"In the library working on a paper. I didn't go to class or back to my room till dinnertime." He raised his chin. "I had no idea anybody was looking for me. Christ."

"And last night?"

That odd expression again. "I was there. In my room by myself. I was supposed to drive down this weekend to see her. I promised." He threw an agonized glance toward Pedersen and then darted toward him another quick look, less readable.

The boy was concealing something. Or was he lying? "So you saw your mother last—when?"

"I guess—it must have been about three weeks ago."

"Do you have any idea who might have done this to her?"

"No!" The word burst from him. "Why would anybody? She was just a . . . an ordinary woman living by herself, not doing anybody any harm. Acting in some plays. I don't think she even had any close friends here.

35

She certainly didn't know anyone who hated her. She's only lived in Bay Cove a few years. It would have had to be . . ." He stopped.

"Yes?"

"I don't know." Again the fleeting expression.

"Was she seeing anyone, Mr. Ashe—any man?"

"Call me Nick. If she was she kept it a secret from me." An expression of puzzlement crossed his face. "She told me after her last divorce she'd had all she wanted of men," he said. He stopped. "She didn't mean me."

"So far as you know, she wasn't intimately associated with anyone in town. How about outside? Did she keep in touch with her last husband?"

"Or my father?" His mouth twisted. "As far as I knew, she wasn't seeing either of them. She talked on the phone to my father sometimes, but he's remarried and . . ." He closed his eyes. His face was drained of color. "Do you have to ask me any more questions now?" He opened his eyes and ran his hand over his face.

"They can wait. Where will you be staying?"

"Oh. You'll have to give me the keys. I forgot mine."

"Keys?"

"To the house. My mother's house."

"The house is sealed, Nick. It was the scene of a crime—it's still being processed. You can't enter it yet."

Nicholas Ashe's eyes were frightened. "But I have to. I won't touch anything you don't want me to touch."

"I'm sorry, it's out of the question for another day or so. Do you need a place to stay, is that it? We can help you arrange that."

"No, no. I have to . . . pick up something I need. I'll just be a minute. It is my mother's house, after all."

"I understand that. We'll walk you through tomorrow, or if you'll give us a description of the thing you need, perhaps we can have it picked up for you."

Nicholas stared at him; then he sagged in his chair. He

looked exhausted. "Never mind," he muttered. "I'll get it later."

"Surely one of your mother's friends would put you up overnight," Pedersen said, as Nicholas stood to leave.

The young man shrugged irritably. "I don't really know any of them—to me they're just faces. Anyway, I'd rather be alone. I don't want to talk; I just want to sleep. If I can. I'll get a room at the Shoreline Inn. They always have vacancies." He stopped at the door. "I talked to my dad. He's coming." He attempted a smile. "Don't worry about me."

As the door closed, Pedersen shook his head. *Don't worry about me.* It reminded him of the time Matthew had broken off with his girl and ended up reassuring his father that it would be okay, everything would be okay.

He sighed. Something disturbed him about the boy. Whatever he wanted from that house, he wanted pretty badly. First thing tomorrow he'd recheck the place; the crime scene team was finished—they'd dusted for prints, vacuumed, photographed, gone through the house for evidence. But except for picking up the address book from her desk, he had not looked the place over himself. That was a thing he liked to do alone. Some of his eccentricities were tolerated.

He picked up the square black address book. First thing tomorrow. Then he'd get on to the friends. And husbands.

It had been a long day. He wrapped the cold cheeseburger in a napkin and tossed it in the wastebasket. As he left the room, he thrust a hand into his left jacket pocket, where he kept the green jade worry beads. They relaxed him. Running them comfortingly back and forth through his fingers as he walked to the car, he reflected that he might well have need for them on this case.

CHAPTER FOUR

Tuesday morning had brought the beginnings of order to Pedersen's office. The clutter on his desk had been neatly shoveled to one side and a stack of reports, edges squared off, precisely placed in the center of the desk's surface.

Ronald Tate was the man Pedersen relied on for detail. Five years earlier, Tate had come onto the investigation team, a tall, bony man with wire-rimmed glasses, who looked less like a policeman than a scholar—Chaucer's Clerk, Freda said. Until then, Pedersen had supervised all the detail of a case. Tate freed him. With quiet compe-

tence, Tate gathered information from witnesses, per-
suaded harried technicians to move reports through
swiftly, scheduled the investigation of minutiae. He
checked, rechecked, oiled the wheels for Pedersen.

Pedersen himself had never enjoyed that sort of thing.
It was not what homicide was all about. Aside from ran-
dom killings, and even then, murder was a matter of relationships, personalities, aspirations, even something as
intangible as dreams. Freda had always said he should
have gone into psychology, and that aspect of crime did
fascinate him. Detail just got in his way. But it had to be
handled; in detail lay the evidence.

Standing at his desk, Pedersen glanced at the pile of
papers on its surface. Reading the first sheet, he opened
the packet of peanuts he had picked up on his way in and
ate them slowly, a half kernel at a time, as usual checking
for the dwarf his father had, years before when he had
been a small boy, told him was at the center of each. It
was always there. After he had eaten the last two, he
brushed off his fingers and buzzed Tate. "Can you come
in? What's all this on my desk?"

Tate referred to his notebook. "The neighbors. Reports
from Crime Scene. The husbands. The boy's father
comes in on the four-thirty flight—SFO. He's taking a
limo in, staying at Harbor House. The other one, Carr,
checked out of Station Hill Bed and Breakfast early yesterday morning."

Pedersen looked up sharply. "Monday morning? He
was here?"

"Right. Driving a rented Hertz. Mentioned to the clerk
that he was heading for a flight out of San Francisco.
We've double-checked passenger lists for yesterday, today
and tomorrow—can't seem to find him on any. Checked
the major hotels—hasn't registered. Though," he added,
"if he's a B and B afficionado, he could be in any of a

hundred places. San Francisco's chock-full of them these days."

"And the Coroner's Bureau? The P.M.?"

"Tomorrow everything major should be in. Rand said time of death looked like Sunday evening. Between nine and midnight."

"Between nine and midnight, he thinks?"

Tate nodded and went on. "The autopsy showed that a single blow killed her—massive internal bleeding. Details are there. Oh, and sexual intercourse within hours of death."

"Wonder if that was Carr. What else?"

"The first husband. The boy is pretty fuzzy on him. Says the last name is Creatore. Thinks his mother'd been out of touch with him since her twenties. The son didn't even know about the marriage till pretty recently. His mother told him Creatore works for a newspaper—or runs one—someplace in upstate New York. Shall I follow up?"

Pedersen studied Tate's face absently. "Just get his full name and his address. There can't be many newspaper men named Creatore. Then let's wait on it. It's unlikely." He handed Tate the address book he had picked up the day before. "And let's go through this and talk to local people she knew. Skip"—he slid his notebook from his jacket pocket—"Mullen, Hirsch, Brande, Rabreau. I'll talk to them myself. And I want to talk to the father and to the son again. We can get statements later." He nodded toward the address book. "See what you can find. Whom she was seeing, when they last saw her, how she spent her time."

"Right."

"I'll get back to you later. I'm going over to the house. We won't have to reseal, we're pretty much done there. I just want to get the feel of the place. And find out what Nicholas Ashe was after."

Tate nodded. "That's it?"

"That's it. Get on with the address book. Oh. What did Crime Scene come up with?"

"It's all there." Tate indicated the stack of reports. "They're checking some fibers. They lifted a few clear prints, all hers. Most surfaces were wiped clean or smeared. She must have dusted the furniture the day she died."

"Expecting a visitor. Who came."

"Looks that way."

"Nothing on the murder weapon?"

"Some smears, that's all. It may have been wiped, not too efficiently."

"Find out what it was?"

"Probably something her husband gave her—the art-collecting husband. It's a fetish figure all right. From Nigeria. I spoke to someone at the museum; he said brass and bronze figures like that are used to ensure success in hunting and trading and to protect against disease. They sometimes contain a magical substance like hair from the head of an elder."

"Must have been sitting on her coffee table."

"Yes. A sculpture that size—it's only about ten inches—might have just knocked her out if it hadn't been brass. Brass is heavy, and Rand said she had a thin skull. He said it was a hard blow."

"The sculpture could have dated back to her second marriage as well."

"We can ask Ashe when he gets in. Or the son."

"No, let's hold off for now. Keep it quiet and out of the papers. If they want a weapon, give them something vague. Blunt instrument." Pedersen slid the reports into a folder. "*Not* brass fetish figure."

"One other thing," said Tate. "The phone calls." He indicated the folder. "Four to Chicago in the past two weeks—to the Ashe office. One to Paris two weeks ago.

Carr's number. And half a dozen to Berkeley this week and last. The son."

"Odd. I wonder why the flurry of interest in cast-off husbands." He stood up. "I'm off." He grinned. "Heard from Freda—she's coming back Thursday. Maybe then I can stop eating pizza."

Tate smiled. "My wife would have called that remark an example of male chauvinism."

His superior grunted.

Pedersen broke the seal, unlocked the door, and pushed. Nothing gave. The front door was stuck—swollen, or the house had settled unevenly. He threw his full weight against it. Inside, he checked the back door. That was no more accessible; on the inside jamb of the locked door had been pasted a reminder: KEY LOST. (A reminder to whom? Guests? Herself?) The dead bolt required a key both inside and out. It was the house of a woman without a man. He wondered how she had gotten in and out of the place.

But it was a pleasant house, warm-looking, even with chalk marks and the dark stain on the floor and the silent, curtained rooms. The furniture looked as though it had been picked up along the way, probably accumulated through her several marriages. The pieces were uncoordinated, yet not at odds with one another. A fat shabby armchair sat opposite a sleek black leather one; over the sofa some sort of Oriental spread had been tossed. Chairs and sofa had been placed around a low round coffee table that called to mind his mother's dining room. In the middle of it, daisies in a blue bowl were beginning to wilt.

The desk, even to his untutored eye, looked like a fine piece and glowed with polish. He walked over and opened it. Inside, compartments and cubbyholes were stuffed with papers, which had crumpled as she forced them in. With care, he seated himself on the small chair before the desk. It offered little that surprised him. Bills, some scrawled PAID and dated, some still owing; letters; lists. In his opinion, all women were list makers—another male chauvinist observation, no doubt. A crumpled grocery list suggested she had entertained:

> fumé blanc
> havarti
> Melba toast
> grapes
> p. towels
> sk. milk
> chicken breasts

Another bore reminders:

> mend bl. blouse
> cancel golf Tues.?
> call Simone
> make blitz küchen

Today was Tuesday. He wondered whether she had canceled the appointment and noted the small vanity in the inclusion of the accent and the umlaut. Did, in fact, *kuchen* take an umlaut? He thought back to his high school German. It didn't. He smiled. Funny contradiction in a woman so casual about replacing a lost key.

For the most part the letters were from women friends—breezy or rambling, full of references to people known in common, to volunteer activities, to their grown children's unique living arrangements or problems finding work. He noted a few names and addresses. Nothing here from the son.

And no diary. But an engagement pad lay hidden, caught, stuffed back under a drawer. He opened it to the day of her death. She had made two notes, one in ink,

43

one in pencil, apparently written at different times:
          Nicky
          JC

He flicked back to Saturday. Three notes:
          Rehearsal 10:30
          Lunch P
          JC/pm

The first two notes were tidy, the third scrawled—penciled in haste. He turned ahead to Monday. It was blank, as though she had known she would no longer be present to buy havarti, bake kuchen, mend blouses. Nothing on Tuesday. Her golf dates had been canceled for all time.

He slipped the pad into his pocket.

The bedroom looked out onto a patio facing south. He slid back the heavy curtains, admitting the morning light, and looked around. She had been a woman of casual habits. A soft blue robe lay across the bed, a satin gown in the same shade crushed into a ball on top of it. A pair of high-heeled shoes, made up mostly of thin red straps, had been dropped in the middle of the white fur rug beside her bed, a dress pulled inside out and hung carelessly over a chair back. Her dressing table was littered with cosmetics in expensive-looking jars, crumpled pink tissues, bottles of perfume with French names he didn't recognize and an American one he recalled from television ads. Face down on her bedside table lay an open novel, a best-selling murder mystery set in the Middle Ages, a book Freda had been nagging him to read so they could discuss it.

He opened the dresser drawers. In one, undergarments—slips, bras, panties, filmy and lace-trimmed—lay in slightly tumbled stacks. Under them a checkbook and an envelope containing two twenty-dollar bills. In another drawer, two empty handbags, some scarfs and belts. A third held hose and a jewel case with several pieces that appeared to be of value.

44

The wardrobe revealed a preference for color and a fondness for shoes: a tall transparent plastic cabinet contained pair after pair, mostly high-heeled and bright as a child's paint box. He checked pockets. A ticket stub. A crumpled handkerchief. An old grocery list. Nothing.

An overnight bag on a shelf held several objects. A small framed picture of a square-jawed man in his thirties; across the corner, *All my love, Roger*. A folding travel alarm clock with an inscription: *To Paris! Sally from Roger*. A menu from a New Orleans restaurant. Several old theater playbills. Three poems typed on yellowed paper, signed *Tip*. A stuffed panda and a thick bundle of snapshots. He pocketed the photographs.

The dusty clutter of a storage closet off the hall appeared to have been undisturbed for quite a time. No object had been slipped under or among the stacks of thick colored towels in the linen closet. In the bathroom, nothing—Mercurochrome, aspirin, a three-year-old bottle of antibiotic tablets. No hypochondriac, not that it mattered now. He glanced over the shelves: toothpaste, scented bath powder, hand lotion, all the things he might have expected to find in the bathroom of a woman who cared about her body. A slight scent of cologne still hung in the air. He dumped out the hamper. Nothing but soiled clothing. He crammed the soft garments back into the basket.

Somehow the house surprised him. For a woman who must have lived a rich life, Sally Robinson had a singularly meager accumulation of mementos. Wary? Unsentimental?

But not totally unsentimental. In the guest bedroom, finally, he found what he had been seeking; a shoebox bound by a thick rubber band had been pushed behind a large suitcase. When he slid the elastic off, the box burst open, spilling letters over the floor. He stuffed them back, two bundles held by rubber bands, one tied with a frayed shoelace and dozens more, loose. Putting the box aside, he finished his search and then, tucking it under his arm, let himself out of the house. As he forced the door into place, he thought back on those rows of pert colored shoes. He would like to have met Sally Robinson.

Experience had taught Carl Pedersen the use of surprise—an unexpected knock at a front door, a casual appearance in a garden on a sunny morning, an abrupt request at a reception room desk.

He divided the list of people he himself wanted to visit into three major groups: local friends, Players, husbands. As he had jotted the third heading in his notebook, he thought of Freda. Later in the week, as they lay together in the dark, he would tell her about this list. He would hear the amusement in her voice as she made some remark about the husbands, maybe saying she should try that sort of thing herself, thirty-two years with the same man—and a policeman at that—being a hard cross to bear. Male chauvinist, hell. He wished she were on her way home now, and it had nothing to do with pizza.

He found Eileen Brande at a symphony rehearsal. From the end of the poorly lit corridor, he watched her approach. Violin case in hand, head down, she moved purposefully.

As she came abreast of him, he stepped forward. "Mrs. Brande. Detective Carl Pedersen." He flipped open his identification folder.

She stopped, startled.

"Where can we talk, Mrs. Brande?"

She frowned. "I'm just going in to rehearsal."

"I've spoken with the orchestra director."

"Oh." He watched her examine his face. "There's the lounge—if no one's in there."

"I'm sure," he said, as they seated themselves in the

empty room, "you know why I want to speak with you."

She sighed, a whisper of sound. "Sally."

"Yes. I'd like to have any information that you can give me about her—anything."

"What sort of information? Surely . . ." She was silent for a moment. "Couldn't you just ask questions? I really don't know what you want."

"First, just anything." He smiled. "As the psychoanalysts say, anything that comes into your mind."

An expression of alarm skittered across her face. "I've only known Sally a couple of years—less, really. Let's see. She's around fifty. She's been married three times. She has a son—by her second marriage, that is. She's in the Players group, she folk-dances . . ."

He broke in. "Mrs. Brande, we have factual information of that sort. What I'd like to know from you is how she seemed to you lately—her state of mind, men she might have been seeing, anything unusual she may have mentioned to you."

Silence.

"How did you come to know her?"

"I think we met at a party. Yes. She and I and another friend."

"Mrs. Hirsch?"

She darted a glance at him. "Yes."

"Go on."

"That's all. We got to talking about places we'd been and found we'd all lived in Chicago at some point, and we'd all been to the Greek islands."

"What sort of person was Miss Robinson?"

She thought. "She was a . . . cheerful person. Oh, she worried about little things—her weight, her son . . ."

"What worried her about her son?"

"It wasn't anything serious. The sorts of things all divorced mothers worry about—whether she'd done him

47

damage, whether he'd forgiven her for leaving his father. Why he didn't have a girlfriend."

"Did they appear to have a good relationship?"

"You don't think Nicky. . . ?"

"We don't think anything, Mrs. Brande. We're trying to get a picture of Miss Robinson. If we're to find out who killed her, we need to know who and what was important to her, what was going on in her life. Was the relationship with her son a tense one?"

"Tense? I wouldn't say tense. They had their ups and downs, all mothers and their children do. I think it was a perfectly . . . ordinary relationship."

"Did she worry that he was gay?"

"Why should you think that? Is he?"

"You mentioned the absence of girlfriends. He's a good-looking young man. I should think the ladies would find him attractive." He paused. "Or perhaps it's the young men."

Her face became stern. "I never had the idea she worried about that. Anyway, I've seen them together just a couple of times. How could I possibly know?"

"He didn't come down here very often?"

"That's not what I said. I said *I* hadn't seen them together often."

He met her indignation with a smile. "What about her former husbands? Did she ever see them?"

"If she did, she didn't tell us about it."

"Us?"

"My friend Zora and me. Mrs. Hirsch. The three of us used to do things together. You know, I really didn't know Sally intimately."

"Would you know if she was seeing anyone—a man? Or men?"

She raised her head in a quick movement. "Did you find something in her house that indicated . . . that?" Her voice was sharp.

He watched her face. "I'm asking the questions, Mrs. Brande."

She flushed. "I know. I jus: thought . . . people leave things around."

"What sorts of things?"

"Oh . . . letters."

"We have her engagement pad."

She said nothing.

"Did Sally Robinson see someone—a man, that you know of?"

Her head was down again. "Women our age don't see many men."

"But did Sally Robinson?"

She stiffened and looked up. "Really, Mr. . . . Detective Pedersen, I know nothing at all of Sally's personal life. And I must get to the rehearsal. I'd like to help you, but I can't." She stood. It was a dismissal.

Oh, I think you could, Pedersen remarked to himself as he rose. "I may call on you again," he said. "You have been most helpful." He left her looking after him, an expression of uncertainty on her small features.

He grinned. She was worrying what she had said that he found so helpful.

As he left the room, he glanced back once more. She had raised her hand to her brow in an odd little gesture, as though her head hurt.

CHAPTER FIVE

Damn, Zora thought, damn, *damn,* I've hit the traffic. Another half hour, maybe hour, and the morning commuters would have been over the hill. But she had been restless to be on her way, and Tuesday traffic wasn't usually this heavy.

Silicon Valley and its industry had ruined the winding highway for her. Two years earlier she had swept along the road through sunlight dappled by redwoods, slowing as the turquoise lakes like teardrops slipped by and gazing across the hills to the houses set neatly on their slopes like toys. Now the concentration required just to get across the hill intact made it all but impossible for her to turn her eyes from the windshield.

A black Mercedes suddenly slid in before her; with difficulty she avoided hitting the brake. Close behind loomed a menacing semi. Her back ached with tension.

She looked at her watch. The news would be on in a few minutes. The day before she had been with a customer in Carmel, helping decide on old rugs for a new house. Driving home late, she had slid the radio dial to a local music station and allowed the plaintive melodies of a folk program to fill the car—a day without news, without confirmation of the world's disasters.

But two days on the road—Carmel yesterday, San Francisco today—was too much driving. By evening she would be exhausted. She glanced across the highway. The two lanes going south were almost empty. At this hour the coast road would have been like that. She should have known enough to take it.

The weekly trip to San Francisco had its irony. It gets me out of town, she told herself, but it brings back all those things I don't want to remember, all those years of life in cities. How long, she wondered in a moment of flooding despair, how long can one go on mourning? Isn't it ever over, done with?

She forced herself to turn her mind to the day ahead. In every way, this weekly trip was impossible. In the parking structure it meant snaking up and up in search of an empty place not hemmed in by posts. In the warehouse it meant hours of plodding through the showrooms with their stacks of Aubussons, Persians, Turkomans, Caucasians, their little locked rooms of Nains. The rugs were too heavy for her to lift by herself, and it often took trips to several sources before she found the exquisitely faded little prayer rug from Ghiordes, the ingenuous weaving done by Egyptian children, the strikingly fresh Polish piece. She had a sharp eye for what appealed to her Bay

Cove clientele. The rugs were exciting; the buying of them something altogether different.

And lunch would mean joining the other blank-faced diners waiting in dull compliance for a table. These days even the good restaurants off Michigan Avenue left floors uncarpeted and ceilings unsoundproofed to hurry patrons on their way and free the tables. The Almighty Dollar, as always. But even a carefully prepared, delicately seasoned meal, such as she could never find in Bay Cove, would not offset the sharp irritation she would feel.

She started. Michigan Avenue—what was she thinking? Michigan Avenue was in Chicago. She had a moment of confusion. This had happened before, this confusion of another city with San Francisco. In addition to tension, the return to the city brought upon her a strange sense of unreality, of broken connections. No link had been forged between her snug life in Bay Cove and her earlier urban one; each hung uneasily in time.

One problem this morning was that she had skipped last week's San Francisco trip in order to lunch with Eileen. Missing a trip always made the next one seem longer, more tedious. But Eileen had been able to meet only on that day, and Eileen was one of her few acquaintances in Bay Cove.

Not making friends in Bay Cove had, of course, been deliberate. She had made the decision: she would not bare herself to the risks of closeness. Her one experience of loss and its pain had bitten too deep.

Nothing before had so affected her; even her parents' deaths had not touched her. Her mother, a narcissistic beauty forever before a mirror, had been remote, dutiful, always a little taken aback at her daughter's being there at all, as if she rediscovered the fact of her motherhood each time Zora entered the room. Her father she loved with a sort of desperation. He was a tall, craggy man, complex, generous, not altogether dependable, with a sly sense of humor and a rigid sense of principle. He confused her. She had never understood how to please him, and that had tormented her as a small child. Later she had withdrawn from the effort to win him, but around him always she found herself edgy, unable to relax. Much as she had longed for his acceptance, his death had not stirred the surface of her life. Nor had her mother's. She now knew it was not from an incapacity to mourn.

In Bay Cove she had decided life would be different. And by the time the last workman closed the door on her remodeled house, her life had taken a new shape. The move had been another beginning, this time without attachments. It was a truism: no commitment, no pain. She had instead sought small impersonal pleasures—the rim of purple hills, the glint of bay below in the morning sun, the warm little courtyard restaurant scented by yeasty bakery fragrances where she sat over coffee and a croissant. She felt contentment, not joy. Joy was a two-sided coin. Always a part of her stood off, aloof, removed. Safe.

With Sally and Eileen, finally, tentatively, she had allowed herself the rapport of an undemanding relationship. When they placed the ad, back in August, she had enjoyed the sense of playful conspiracy, the beginnings of friendship. Then, unexpectedly, at the outset of their adventure, the thread that bound them pulled loose. For the past weeks she had met each of them alone, and Eileen and Sally had not met at all.

Traffic was now crawling. In an effort to relieve the tension along her spine, she pulled her shoulders back hard; it didn't help. Ahead, the wooded summit glinted green in the sunlight. She checked the time. Eight-thirty-five already. She reached for the radio dial. From the rear speakers the rich strains of Brahms's *Alto Rhapsody* poured into the car. She adjusted the volume and found a news station. ". . . Fair with a weather front moving in." Too late. She switched back to music, slowing for the laboring van that had moved in front of her. She gritted her teeth. Her jaw ached. Her back ached. She needed a toilet.

The summit achieved, the van shot off with frightening abruptness. She gripped the wheel, wishing she were anywhere but here. But at San Jose the road widened and emptied slightly. A little farther along she found a rest stop.

In the city, finally, she swung off at the downtown exit. As she entered the parking structure, the music from the speakers grew muffled. She turned the radio off and faced the day.

The day had been exhausting. It was with relief that she reclaimed her car. The back of the station wagon heavy with her purchases, she pulled into the highway going south. The evening exodus had not yet begun. She'd be home before five.

The radio was still set to the music station. She glanced at her watch and spun the radio dial. Without preamble, the words came from the speakers behind her: ". . . concerning university employee and amateur actress Sally Robinson, former wife of the noted art dealer James Freeman Carr the Third. She was found dead yesterday morning in her Bay Cove home, victim of an assault. Police have ruled out burglary as a motive. . . . And today in San Francisco . . ." She snapped off the radio and found she was trembling so she could barely hold the wheel.

For four years she had maintained her detachment. In a single day it had crumbled.

The road ahead looked interminable.

CHAPTER SIX

"Eileen, you poor thing," Zora said. "What on earth did he ask? What did you tell him?" She lit a cigarette from the one she had just smoked.

They had angled their chairs close to Zora's fireplace and sat before the flames that flicked soft tongues over the madrone. Their wineglasses were full, the fire and the lighted lamps warmed the October dusk that lay on the room, but the ambience was lost on them. Both sat forward in their chairs, their bodies rigid with tension.

"Nothing," Eileen said. "I didn't tell him anything. I

mean nothing that . . ." She left the sentence incomplete. "God, my head is splitting. It's all just so *awful*."

"I know. Today on the way home—well. Do they know what happened? Did he tell you what they'd found? How she died?"

"No. When I asked, he said *he* was asking the questions. I can't remember very clearly. He startled me, and then I kept remembering that I was missing rehearsal. Besides, I've been upset all day. It's so crazy—Sally wasn't the sort of person people kill. I can't imagine anyone's wanting to kill her."

Zora nodded. "I know." After a while she said, "They always think of family. Family members kill each other."

"There's her son and all those husbands. No." Eileen shook her head once, vigorously, then stopped as though it hurt. "Not her son. The police wouldn't . . . that's . . . no."

"There's that man we met through *Happy Times*."

"Paul? Honestly, Zora! Anyway, we decided not to see him."

"I know that, but before we decided, we never really got to know anything about him. And Sally—"

Eileen frowned. "Did Sally say something?"

"No, she didn't say anything. But—"

"Well then." Eileen reached for Zora's poker and gave the fire a jab. "I think you're all wrong. Paul seemed to me an awfully decent guy, warning us about the trouble we could get into, doing what we were. And Sally never kept anything to herself in her life. If she'd been seeing him, we'd know it."

Zora shook her head. "The only other possibility I can think of is a break-in. She could have interrupted a burglar."

"The paper said nothing had been stolen."

"Maybe he hit her and got scared and ran."

"Maybe," she said dubiously. "No, that can't be." She

rose and went to the magazine rack to poke among the copies of the *Wall Street Journal*. "Don't you take the *Banner*?"

"Sometimes I pick it up. I never got one yesterday, I was in Carmel all day."

Eileen returned to her chair. "That's where you were? I tried and tried to get you on the phone."

"You could have called the shop. They always know where I am."

"I didn't think. Anyway, yesterday's paper said it wasn't a burglary. I can't remember how they knew." She ran her hand over her face. "Do you have a couple of aspirins?"

"I'm sorry. My head's so full of . . ." Zora returned with aspirin and a glass of water.

"Thanks, that'll help. Anyway, I didn't tell the detective about the *Happy Times* ad or about Paul. And I don't think you should. If he ever gets around to talking to you, that is."

"Oh, my turn's coming. There was a message at the shop when I got in this afternoon. He's coming by here tomorrow morning." She drew on her cigarette. "What's it like being interviewed by a detective?"

"Awful. He acted as though he knew all sorts of dire things about me. And he wouldn't answer a single question of mine."

Zora looked at her thoughtfully. "And you didn't even mention Paul?"

Eileen rose and began to pace behind Zora's chair. "Think what it might do to him. If Paul's a perfectly innocent bystander, why put him through that—get his name in the papers, who knows what else. And our names, too—have you thought of *that*? How would you like having everyone in town know what we did? We'll look like . . . perverts or something."

57

Zora laughed uneasily. "Not perverts. But silly women, I grant you."

"It would do your business no good."

"No."

"Nor me with the orchestra."

"I know."

Eileen returned to her chair. She picked up her glass and finished her wine. "I have to go. You know, Zora, I've been feeling sick over the whole thing. The whole *Happy Times* business, fighting over Paul, now Sally's murder and that detective creeping around. Who knows what sorts of things he'll find out. I hate it all. I just like to be"—she sought the precise word—"unobtrusive, and now look what's happened." She sounded as though she might cry.

Zora extended her hand. "Don't be so upset. I'm sure you can still be unobtrusive. And of course you feel bad—what sort of friend would you be if you didn't?"

"That's it, she wasn't really my friend any longer. And if we tell that detective about the *Happy Times* thing, we won't have a chance of being unobtrusive. You won't tell him, Zora, will you?"

"I won't. I mean I won't swear not to, if for some reason I should have to, but I won't volunteer anything. I won't, Eileen—relax."

Relax, Eileen thought as she took her jacket from Zora. She felt bitter.

The aspirin hadn't helped and she was late. Paul would be waiting for her at their restaurant.

Alone, Zora returned to her chair by the fire. She was tired and depressed. Eileen was luckier than she knew; at least her interview was over. And Eileen seemed so sure of what to say. Or what not to say.

But when you came right down to it, what was there to say? Until the evening they wrote the ad, she had

58

known no more of Sally than that she was an amusing person, available for an occasional movie or dinner. It was Sally's very lightness that had attracted her, Sally's way of skimming the surface of life like a skater delighting in the ice beneath her skates, sure that it would never break and drop her into frigid waters. Sally's had been a different sort of detachment from her own.

Of course—the ice had broken.

And she had agreed not to mention Paul. She wondered how good this detective was at his job. She was a poor liar.

CHAPTER SEVEN

Pedersen found the letter Nicholas Ashe was seeking where Sally Robinson had concealed it, slipped into the yellowing envelope of a ten-year-old note from her mother. She had hidden it, probably from herself, but she could not throw it away. He had seen behavior like this before, in the parents of teenage drug users, in the families of young rapists. It was shame, shame and fear, that motivated them to self-deception. If they could avoid looking, if they could pretend, perhaps it would all go away.

The message was unclear and the tone was odd; the letter was confused, disconnected, ambivalent:

Dear Mother,

This letter is painful to write and I imagine will be painful to read. I wouldn't have written it at all if I hadn't absolutely had to. I'd have just kept quiet about the whole thing.

But something may happen, and I want you to be prepared. If it does, if someone calls or comes and tells you things about me, I want you to know they're not true. And I want you to ask Dad not to cut me off. I don't care anymore what you two think of me, but I do need Dad's help till I'm out of school and on my own.

You were always on my case about finding a girlfriend—well, you may not like what happened as a result. But you'll be glad to know I have (or maybe the word is had) what you call a relationship. So you see I'm perfectly normal, after all.

Of course, Mother, I don't think you wanted me to have a girl for me at all, but just to prove to yourself that I have no problems, which makes you a good mother. What I feel about myself has never mattered to you, only what you feel about yourself.

I'm sorry about this. I know you have enough trouble accepting me as it is, and Dad's all occupied with his new family and doesn't really care anymore.

I figure this will be the final disappointment for both of you. Dad has always wanted me to be strong, even when you two were casually blasting

my life apart, and I just am not what he wants or
you want.

> *Your loving son,*
> *Nick*

He read it twice, shaking his head. *Your loving son.*

As he sat holding it, Ronald Tate came in. "No peanuts? Not even worry beads?"

Pedersen himself found it strange that he, a big man—large bones, large hands, large feet—so liked small things. Succulents, for example. Freda was inclined toward brilliant flowers with tissue-like textures. Anemones. Ranunculuses. Iceland poppies. He, on the other hand, was quite contented with a corner here, a bit of wall there, in their backyard for the tiny sedum he loved in its various and unspectacular forms. He guessed the peanuts—small, complex, with their dwarfs at the centers—were like that. As were the worry beads, purchased in the Plaka of Athens on his and Freda's one vacation abroad: quarter-inch jade-like cylinders with rusty markings, strung like a child's bracelet, which he kept in his left jacket pocket, transferring them as he changed clothing. He knew nothing about the origins of their use, but he found rolling them through his fingers a solace when he was stuck, mulling a case.

And Freda, he added to himself, with a mental grin—did even she belong in a class with the succulents, the worry beads, the peanuts? No one had ever attracted him as Freda had—tiny, small-boned, graceful, totally feminine yet without an unnecessary ounce of flesh, the antithesis of the image he had always associated with the name Freda, the German hausfrau. But Freda was no mere pretty little woman. Her sense of herself was sharp and sure. Nothing diminutive about that.

He turned his attention back to Tate. "See what you think of this." He handed him the letter.

62

Tate read. "He's into something. Drugs?"

"Maybe—doesn't feel right, though. I think it's something else. Whatever it is, he wanted to get to this letter before we did. He'd never have found it." He showed Tate where it had been concealed. "This must be the reason for all the phone calls to Berkeley. And the favorite coffee cake."

"Coffee cake?"

"Just something a neighbor said. How's it going?"

"Fine. Did you pick up anything else?"

"This." He handed Tate the engagement pad. "She never used a name when an initial would do—economical with her time, this lady. It may give us some information. See what you turn up." He stood up. "What about Carr—come up with anything yet?"

"Still checking."

"I'll leave you the rest of these letters—you may find something. The one bundle is early stuff—a couple signed Tip, from the first husband, I think. The thin bundle is letters from Carr, written when they were married and he was making trips to Europe. The other letters are from her parents. Both deceased. I've looked at all the loose letters—nothing." He stood up. "Enjoy."

"You're going to The Players?"

"Right. All the aspiring amateurs in town seem to have known Robinson. I'll catch Mullen there and maybe the mysterious Simone, whoever she is."

"They know you're coming?"

"No, I phoned to find out rehearsal time, but I didn't identify myself. I'd imagine they'll be expecting me by now, though—Robinson was to have been in this new production."

"What about the other woman friend?"

"Hirsch? The people at her shop say she's gone into San Francisco—some wholesale house, a buying trip. She

63

was in Carmel all day yesterday. I'll get her tomorrow—I left a message."

At the door, he stopped. Tate waited.

"Which is better, sirloin or . . . I thought when Freda came in—never mind, I'll ask the butcher."

As the door closed, Tate grinned.

The Players operated out of an old barn at the edge of town. It had been given to them by their first and only angel, the woman who had started the civic theater group.

The place was easy to spot. Plastered on one side, orange banners proclaimed in purple letters the virtues of the coming play: NOTHING BEFORE LIKE IT, THE TOTAL DRAMATIC EXPERIENCE, FIRST TIME IN THE BAY AREA. Pedersen wondered if it was one of those touchy-feely audience participation things he hated.

The outer structure was essentially unchanged from its origin as a farm building. Inside, a box office and a counter for the intermission sale of coffee and soft drinks were separated from the theater proper by a wall. Beyond that, Pedersen knew, three shallow tiers of seats wrapped a small stage.

The entrance area was empty, but Pedersen could hear someone shouting instructions. "Spot on *her*. Drop the lights on the rest of the stage. That's it. Go ahead, Laura. He's just walked out."

As Laura began to speak, Pedersen edged in and took a seat in the shadows. The man who had been shouting was a stocky, balding figure, wearing a shirt of some exotic fabric (African? Pedersen wondered) partially covered by a knee-length woolen garment that suggested his intent to herd goats in the near future. Below worn jeans, his feet were clad in dirty Birkenstock sandals.

Things seemed to be going awry. Laura had stopped speaking and the balding man appeared to be on the verge of a seizure of some sort. "Oh, fuck! No, no, *no,* Laura, not like *that.* You're not desolated. You hate the guy's guts. You're rid of the shit—you're taking in the fact that the bastard's really out of your life. But it means hassles over the kids and money and going back to work. You have mixed emotions—*mixed,* get it, babe?—mixed. Love-hate?"

Pedersen looked around. The theater was almost empty. Those people present sat within the small ring of diffused light from the spot, intent on Laura's performance. The balding man must be Mullen—Louis Mullen, The Players' director.

Someone coming in stumbled against him.

"When do they take a break?" Pedersen whispered.

"Any minute now. When he begins to have tantrums, it means he wants his lunchtime martini." The boy grinned. "Waiting for somebody?"

"I need to talk with Mr. Mullen."

"Better catch him right away." He moved on past.

"Okay," Mullen barked. "That's more like it. Okay, let's stop while we're ahead." He looked at his watch. "Break till two-thirty."

Pedersen caught him as he was heading backstage. "Mr. Mullen. Just a minute, please."

Mullen swung around without stopping, a scowl on his face. "Not now," he said with irritation. "Who the hell are you?"

"Now, I'm afraid, Mr. Mullen. Police. Detective Pedersen."

Mullen stopped and peered uncertainly at Pedersen's identification. "I figured someone would be along." He sighed. "Can we do this in my office?"

Pedersen followed him into the windowless cubicle.

"Drink?" Mullen was uncapping a Thermos with an air of urgency. "Martini," he elaborated.

Pedersen shook his head. "Can we close this door?" He

gave it a shove and seated himself on the only uncluttered chair. Mullen swung himself up on the desk, one hand flat on its surface, the other nursing the Thermos cap he was using as a cup, his feet in their grimy sandals swinging. Pedersen took out his notebook. "Let's start with a little information on you."

Mullen was sixty-one, not currently married. He was childless. He lived at an address Pedersen knew to be near the beach, a low-rent area.

"The phone's unlisted," Mullen said, after he had given his number.

"We noticed. Actors bother you at night?"

"The actors—at night?" Mullen laughed. "Most nights I'm here and the cast's here, too. No, I was getting crank calls"—he smiled—"at inconvenient moments. Then, too," he added, "I have this ex-wife." He seemed to regard the explanation as complete.

Pedersen gave him a man-to-man nod of understanding, his spirits taking a little leap at the word *wife*. Uxorious, that's what he was, no doubt about it. Freda had introduced him to the word. "What can you tell me about Sally Robinson?"

"Sally. What can I tell you? She was a good little actress, that I can tell you. Sexy little broad, too." He studied Pedersen's face. "I had this little thing with her, although . . ." He glanced uneasily toward the door. "I'd as soon the others didn't know. It didn't go anyplace, anyway. She was looking for something—long-term, I guess, and that's not my bag."

"Love 'em and leave 'em," Pedersen remarked. "Slam, bam, thank you, ma'am?"

Mullen reddened. "That's not it. It's just that I've had one bout with marriage—and bout's the word. A K.O. in the first round and I was the one on the ropes. Now right at the outset I let the ladies know where I stand. If they're interested, it's their party—or funeral—or whatever the hell they regard it as. But if they're looking to me for commitments, I ease out early."

"And Sally? She was looking for commitment?"

"I thought so. You sense these things. Anyway, our . . . friendship reached what you might call fruition only once. She wasn't having any. Nice little piece in the sack, but"—he waved the hand with the Thermos cap—"it wasn't in the cards. No hard feelings, of course," he added. He grinned and poured another martini. "I didn't finish the lady off in a jealous rage or a fit of frustration."

"Have you any notion as to who might have done so?"

"I certainly do *not*. In fact, that's one of the things that struck me—she wasn't the sort of woman to make enemies. She was easygoing, easy to get along with; in fact, I guess you'd say the word *easy* describes her best. Everybody liked her." He looked away. "Almost everybody."

"Who didn't like her?"

"I didn't say anyone didn't."

"It occurred to you that someone doesn't quite love Sally Robinson."

Mullen shrugged. "It's unimportant. I thought of Simone—she wasn't wild about Sally."

"And who is Simone? Tell me about her."

"Simone Rabreau. She was the lead in our last play. Did you see *The Ledge*?"

"Yes." Pedersen tried to remember what it had been about.

"Simone was the younger woman the guy was going to marry. Remember, he left Sally and the kid for this thirty-five-year-old woman?"

"Seems to be a popular theme in your plays."

Mullen looked blank. "Oh. You mean Laura today. A whole different bag—come see it when we open."

"We always do." Freda was committed to civic theater. "And why did Simone not like Sally?"

67

Mullen developed a sudden interest in the design of the Thermos cap. "It's . . . she and I have this . . ."

"Thing?" supplied Pedersen.

"Mmm, this thing going at the moment. I guess she found Sally a little too sexy—with me, that is—to suit her. Sally was a flirtatious woman."

"But nothing was going on between you and Sally. And you make no commitments."

"No, but you know how women are. You have to string them along a little or they just take off. Simone . . ."

"She drew some incorrect conclusions about your relationship and you left it that way."

"For the moment, yes. I'd have straightened things out."

One morning as you got out of bed, Pedersen commented to himself. Out of the sack, that is. He said, "So exactly what was your relationship with Sally at the time of her death?"

"I told you. We were friends, nothing more. I'd made my pitch, we'd given it a try, and she'd brushed me off. No hassle. We didn't needle each other. I liked her. She liked me."

"I see. What were you doing Sunday night?"

Mullen started. "You don't . . . oh, I see. Everybody has to have an alibi."

"No alibi. Just tell me what you did that evening."

"As a matter of fact, I was at a movie Sunday night. With Simone. They were showing an old film, *Lolita,* from Nabokov's book—I'd never seen it. Great piece of acting. Mason handles that role with such delicacy—the dirty old gentleman. The dirty, sad, aristocratic, yearning, *obsessed* old gentleman." His features blurred with emotion. For the first time during their talk, he was moved. "Beautiful. Just *beautiful.*" He recalled himself to

68

the present. "We went back to Simone's afterward. Check with her. She's in the book."

Pedersen didn't have to guess why he had gone to Simone's, but he had been touched by the moment of real feeling in the man. "Do you know anything about the other men in Sally Robinson's life?"

"Did she have any? I know she was divorced. And she had a son—he came one time to watch a dress rehearsal. I don't think she had anybody." Puzzlement crossed his face. "Funny she didn't. Maybe it was her age. Anyway, she never told me about anyone else. Not that she'd have chosen me to tell."

"Mr. Mullen, if you do think of anything else, if anybody else mentions anyone, I'd like you to let me know. I'll give you a number where you can reach me direct."

"Will there be a service for Sally, do you know?" The man's face was troubled. "We'd all want to go."

"Her son and his father are arranging something, I'm sure. Mr. Ashe will be at Harbor House if you want to call."

"Poor kid," Mullen said and then looked embarrassed. "She wasn't a kid, I realize, but she always sort of seemed like one. So . . . enthusiastic." He defended his statement. "It's a young emotion. And she was always so optimistic." He sighed and reached for the Thermos.

As Pedersen opened the office door to let himself out, Mullen was pouring himself a generous third martini. No doubt, Pedersen reflected dryly, to toast the poor kid.

Simone Rabreau lived in an apartment built over a two-car garage at the foot of a driveway. Someone had recently tried to make it look like a cottage, whitewashing the exterior, affixing strips of wood painted black to simulate shutters, filling two homemade window boxes with young geranium plants. The effort had been unsuccessful;

it still looked like a garage. In the upstairs windows he could see stiff white curtains.

Pedersen had not phoned, but his knock immediately produced a shout from above. "Two secs. Hang on, it's locked." In a few minutes she padded down the steps and opened the door, a small woman with the straight flat back of a dancer.

"Oh. I thought you were someone else." Her head was wrapped hugely in a yellow bath towel, her slight body clasped within an oversized white terry-cloth robe. "Who *are* you?" She pulled her sash tighter.

Pedersen introduced himself.

She continued to stand blocking the entrance. "Are you sure it's me you want to talk to?"

"Routine. We're speaking with several Players people."

"I'm sure I don't know what I can tell you." But she smiled suddenly and stepped aside to let him in. The smile altered the sharp little face and filled it with mischief. Involuntarily, Pedersen smiled back.

Simone Rabreau was Gallic in name only. Upstairs the two-room apartment compounded the cottage motif with rag rugs, cotton in large black and white checks, and several pieces of Americana—a handsome weather vane, a doll from some grandmother's attic, a beautifully proportioned handmade rocker. Pedersen seated himself in it.

Simone stood over him, uncertain. "I'll put on some clothes, just be a minute." At the door she turned. "Can I give you something? Tea? Sherry?"

"Tea would be good. Attractive place you have."

Pleasure warmed her face. "Thanks. It's a funky little garage, but I think it's neat. I have a great landlady, too." She sounded young.

The kitchen area was divided off by freestanding shelves. He watched her fill a tea kettle, set it on a burner and leave the room.

"So." Dressed, she sat down opposite him and poured their tea. "What do you want to know?"

"You understand why I'm here—Sally Robinson's death?"

She nodded. "I figured."

"Just tell me anything you think might be helpful. Any special plans she had in the offing, anyone she was seeing, anything in her life different from the usual."

"You know, I don't know her all that well. Have you talked to Lou Mullen?"

Pedersen nodded.

"Maybe she told him something. He knows a lot about all of us. And she . . . liked him."

"Did she have a man friend who picked her up after performances?"

"Nobody I know of—she brought her own car. Sometimes Lou walked her to it, but then he'd come back."

"You say she liked him. Were they romantically involved?"

"Romantically?" She laughed. "That's the wrong word for Lou. But she was always coming on to him—she was that kind of woman."

"She flirted with him?"

"You could call it that. I think they had some little thing going before I was in The Players, but the past year Lou and I have been . . . seeing each other."

"Tell me about Mr. Mullen."

"Lou?" Her face took on a pinched look. "You don't suspect him, do you?"

"Just tell me about him, if you will."

She raised her palms. "What's to tell? He's divorced—down on marriage, in fact. He's a pretty good director when he isn't losing his temper. Which he does a lot." She laughed. "You haven't lived if you haven't experienced Lou in one of his rages." She stopped. "I don't mean—he isn't violent or anything." She threw a sharp

71

glance at him. "It's that business with his wife, isn't it—that's what you wanted to ask me about. That really wasn't his fault, you know. The whole thing just got out of control. He got a suspended sentence."

Pedersen controlled his reaction. "What really happened—as you understand it?"

"The way Lou told me, they'd both been drinking. He was mad and yelling and his wife picked up a coffee mug and threw it at him. It almost knocked him out and he just let her have it. But she was the one who started the whole thing—she had as bad a temper as he did. The only problem was, she got bitchy and turned him in. It scared him. He hasn't ever done anything like that again."

"He told you he hasn't?"

"Not just that. He's really funny—funny peculiar—about violence, seems to be afraid of it. In general, I mean, not just his own temper. He yells a lot, then he gets this funny look all of a sudden and he just calms down. Like that." She snapped her fingers. "You know"—her words were an appeal—"I've seen a lot of Lou this year, and he's really a very gentle guy most of the time."

"He drinks heavily." It was a statement.

"You can say that again." She grinned and relaxed. "He doesn't get drunk, though."

"Did you ever see him lose his temper with Sally Robinson?"

"Oh, sure, he loses it with all of us all the time. When it comes to The Players, he's a real perfectionist. It doesn't mean anything, though." Her grin was engaging. "He says *fuck* a lot and then we go on. He's really an okay guy."

"Let's go back to Sally. Is—was there anything at all in her life that you connect with her murder?"

"Not really. She was pretty mellow—you know,

72

didn't get uptight about things. Most of us liked her. I wasn't all that crazy about her because, well, I told you, she came on to Lou. But she was easy to be around. Maybe the one thing I'd say about her is that she wasn't very careful—maybe I mean cautious. I can imagine her leaving a door unlocked or picking somebody up in her car, stuff like that. She was maybe a little too relaxed. Are you sure somebody didn't just walk in and . . ." She left the thought unfinished.

Not easily he didn't, Pedersen thought, recalling Sally's doors.

"Anyway." She peered into his full cup and then poured herself a second. "I don't have anything else to tell you. I did meet her son. Came to a dress rehearsal. Nice-looking."

"What about Sunday night? There was no rehearsal then, was there?"

"No, Lou does take Sundays off. We went to a movie he'd been wanting to see. *Lolita*. Ever see it? He was very excited about the acting."

Pedersen nodded. "I see. What showing was that, by the way?"

"There's only one Sunday night. It's at eight. It started even later, but that was just as well, Lou was late. They usually run those old films for two nights, but not this time, and Lou really wanted to see it."

"How late was he?"

"Not too. I don't remember exactly." She flicked an uneasy glance his way.

"You and Sally didn't get together outside of The Players?"

"Not really. We had lunch a couple of times to talk about a scene. She was quite a bit older—of course Lou is, too, but that's different.""

"Of course." Pedersen closed his notebook. "If I think of anything else, I'll be in touch with you. If you think of

73

anything, you call me." He handed her a card. "You've helped."

"I don't see how, but thanks. I better get this hair dry. Just slam the door when you go out. It locks."

At the foot of the path he looked back. She was standing at the kitchen window drying her hair and looking after him, the pinched look back on her face.

At the first phone kiosk, he stopped.

"Run a check on our people. It seems Mullen was charged with wife-beating. Suspended sentence. Run one on everybody, just to make sure. You have any luck with matching initials and names?"

Tate sounded smug. "You know what Creatore's given name is? Jocomo."

"J.C."

"Yep, two of 'em. Jocomo Creatore. James Carr."

"She never had to change her monogram."

"There was Ashe in between."

"Right. Probably doesn't mean anything—with Carr in town, those were probably his initials. But you better call this Creatore. See if you think we'll have to go there. New York, was it?"

"Mmm, New York, some little town. I have an address and number for him."

"Good. I'm going to stop for a bite and then I'm going on over to Harbor House to talk to Ashe. Get the Creatore thing out of the way. It's three hours later in New York—he should be home by now. Leave me a report— I'll get back to my desk later."

Creatore, Ashe—by tomorrow it would be two down, one to go. Back in his car, he slowly ate the peanuts he had bought that morning, thinking. By tomorrow he'd know about one of the J.C.'s, but it was the missing J.C.— Carr—that really concerned him. And the elusive P.

CHAPTER EIGHT

Paul was annoyed, that was clear. He hated her being late. And tonight the place was jammed, every table and bar stool filled. To make things worse, a stony-faced waiter she had never before seen was hovering in a way she knew infuriated Paul.

Most nights they liked the place, in part because they had discovered it together. Newly opened, off the beaten track on a dark side street lined with small businesses that closed each night at six, it was one of the few eating places in town that had not yet been touted by the local newspapers. Prices were high and the menu limited, but the chef was a man dedicated to sending forth patrons who would return; it had become a restaurant with a following. For now that was fine, although, as Eileen pointed out, it was just a matter of time before a write-up in *Happy Times* ruined it for them. Most of the good restaurants in town required reservations in advance. Bay Cove's population liked to eat.

"I'm sorry—don't say anything, Paul." Eileen slid into the chair the waiter had pulled out. "I'm on edge as it is, and my head's pounding."

"Do you want a drink?" His voice was cold.

"Just wine—anything. Paul, don't be angry. I just can't cope with it tonight."

He relented. "It's that new waiter. All he can think about is freeing up the table so he'll make another tip. Assembly-line eating—hell of a way to run a restaurant. We'd better look for another place next time."

"If you don't stop glowering like that, there may not be a next time." She forced a laugh.

"I hope it would take more than that. What's the matter? Why are you so upset?"

"What do you think? You haven't totally forgotten Sally, have you? The first of us—remember?"

"Okay, don't get bitchy about it." His eyes were sharply curious. "Was she that close a friend? You never said much of anything about her."

"Does she have to be an intimate friend for me to be upset over her death? She was a friend, that's enough."

"Of course. I feel bad about it, too." He reached across the table for her hand. "I'm sorry—I'm an insensitive boor. You must be disturbed. Have you seen the family—her son or anyone?"

"No." She stopped. "How did you know she had a son?"

He met her eyes. "As you pointed out, we did meet for lunch. We talked about our families."

"Are you sure?" She sat forward in her chair.

"Am I sure? Of course I'm sure." He withdrew his hand. "You and your friend were sitting in the booth behind us; you saw us yourselves."

"I don't mean that." She shook her head, impatient. "I know you met her then. I mean—oh, the devil with it." She picked up her wineglass. "This is my third since five o'clock. Plus aspirin. If I can't drive, please see that I get home." She laughed shortly.

"Don't worry. I always see that my dates get home. You've probably noticed—no leftovers around the place ever."

She was silent.

"All right, not funny. Let's order, and then tell me about it."

Over soup she began to relax. "I was interviewed."

"Interviewed?"

"By a detective. Detective Pedersen. He interrupted rehearsal—well, he didn't exactly interrupt it—to interview me. I haven't the faintest notion what he was fishing for or expecting me to say. He wanted to know Sally's state of mind."

"Did you know her state of mind?"

"Does anybody know anybody else's state of mind? Sometimes I don't even know the state of my own mind. I had thought she seemed anxious about something lately, but I didn't tell him."

"Why not?"

"Because I don't *know*. How can I go telling some policeman a vague impression I had? Besides, it may have been projection on my part."

"Projection? Have you been feeling anxious over something?"

"No. I don't think so. I'm not making sense. It's just that he asked me some pretty odd questions, like whether Nicky, that's her son, is gay and whether they get—got along. Did they have a tense relationship, that's how he put it." She put her spoon down with a clink. "God. What mother doesn't have a tense relationship with her son at least some of the time?"

"Are sons so bad? You seem to enjoy yours."

She laughed. "Speaking of states of mind, I'm not in the jolliest mood myself tonight, am I? Anyway, he asked me other questions. It sounded as though he found something, I don't know what, that indicated she'd had a man around."

Paul signaled and the waiter removed their soup bowls. When the waiter had gone, he said, "Found what?"

She shrugged. "I have no idea."

He looked at her thoughtfully. "What could they find? Besides, what's so odd about an unattached woman having a man around?"

"The police have her engagement pad," Eileen said.

There was a brief silence.

Eileen broke it. "On the way here, I stopped at Zora's. You know who she is?"

He nodded.

"She mentioned you."

"She mentioned *me*? In what way?"

"She said we should tell the police about the *Happy Times* ad. And about you."

"I see." His mouth was tight. "And did she do that?"

"The police haven't talked to her yet. Paul, I asked her not to—in fact, I got her to promise not to. She swore she wouldn't volunteer anything, she'd only tell if she had to."

"That promise does not make me feel completely secure." He looked with distaste at the entree that had been placed before him. "I find I'm not as hungry as I thought."

"I know. I'm sorry I had to tell you, but I was

afraid . . . If Zora does say anything and you didn't know about it . . . it's not just for you I'm worried, it's for all three of us. The ad—that's the sort of thing the *Banner* gobbles up; they have nothing else to write about. What ever happens in this town?"

"Something seems to have happened this time."

"Paul." She put her fork down. "Is this going to make a difference between us?"

"Why should it?" But his voice was strained.

"I'm very attached to you. You know that, don't you?"

"I assumed I was no longer merely a convenient escort."

"I don't think Zora'll say anything, really I don't. And, anyway, you've only seen Sally once in your life. What can anyone make of that?"

He laughed shortly. "What indeed?"

79

CHAPTER NINE

Lou Mullen was late; the tiff erupted over that. Since Lou had never questioned the assumption that the best defense was an offense, as soon as she spoke, he attacked. "You tell me about being late"—he said, before she had—"when we've held up rehearsal because you were still home having your second cup of coffee—"

Simone broke in. "Once. That happened *once,* and I've never heard the end of it. With you it's habitual. You'd be late—"

"—to my own funeral."

She laughed. "Well, you would. Look, Lou, if you'd

just let me know. I wait and wait—there is a phone if you're held up at the Barn. Couldn't you call?"

He refused to answer, rising with great dignity to make his way to her refrigerator. "Beer?" he inquired coldly.

"No. I had some wine while I was waiting."

Over his beer, he relented slightly. "It's been a shitty day all 'round. Some detective came and badgered me about Sally, then we started work later than I had planned this afternoon—it's been like that all day." He rested his head against the chair back.

He looks old tonight, she thought. "He visited me, too," she said.

"He?" He sat up. "The detective? That Pedersen?"

"Mmm. He'd already seen you. Really, all he wanted was to know more about you."

"What sort of more?" He examined her face through narrowed eyes.

"Oh, your marriage and all. I told him you weren't violent."

"You what?" He stood up so suddenly he upset his beer can. "What do you mean you told him I'm not violent? What the fuck did you tell him that for?"

She returned from the kitchen with paper towels and began to mop. "Don't get so excited. It was just about your wife—I told him it wasn't your fault and that your sentence was suspended."

"You didn't!" He groaned. "Well, *thank* you, Simone! Thank you very much. Now he'll be on my tail again, after I thought I'd shaken him. How in God's name did you get on that topic?"

She was crushed. "I didn't get on it. I don't know how it came up. He knew." She hesitated. "I'm sure he knew."

"And just in case he didn't, you let him know."

"Lou—it's like this business of being late. Somehow it

always turns out to be my fault, or whatever it is I do it's worse or more often than you. *I* wasn't late tonight. You were. I wasn't late Sunday night when we saw *Lolita*. You were. I didn't tell that detective anything he didn't know."

The room was still. "What did you say about Sunday night?"

Confused, she examined his face with apprehension. "I said you were late, I wasn't."

"You told that to the detective?"

"No. Of course I didn't. Why would I?"

"I wasn't late, you know."

"Lou, you were so. This is me, Simone. You don't have to lie to me."

"I wasn't late. The film started late."

"Yes, it did, but what does that have to do with it? You were late, too. You came in when the lights were out and you had to crawl over that Hirsch woman who was sitting at the end. Don't you remember? The film had been going on for about fifteen, twenty minutes."

"What Hirsch woman? The rug lady—Sally's friend?"

"Yes. She was there. She didn't notice us, I don't think."

"But if pressed, she'd remember I was late. Is that what you're saying?"

"Lou! What the hell's wrong with you? You make it sound as though I think you were late because you were out bludgeoning Sally."

"No." He bent to blot a puddle she had missed under the table. After a moment, he straightened, his face suffused with color. "No, of course you didn't think that." He reached over to pat her on the knee. "Let's just skip the whole thing. I'm tired. I don't want to argue anymore."

"Neither do I." She rose and bent to kiss him.

He clasped her wrists and pulled her down. "I'm sorry I'm late, babe. Next time I'll call." He slid his hand over her breast. "Dinner now? Or later?"

CHAPTER TEN

Harbor House was Bay Cove's major hotel. The long complex of six-story buildings had been set along the natural curve of the shoreline, making it possible for guests at the more costly north end to watch the surfers, small dauntless figures in shining second skins who mounted breakers that threatened to dash them against jagged rock. Guests to the south overlooked the public beach with its tangled couples and sunning seniors. Below their windows, young mothers in cutoff jeans recovered lost shovels; teenage girls in triangles of colored fabric spread-eagled themselves on the warm sand.

Guests on the bay side could look across to Seal Rock, the stony projection upon which the barking sea lions hurled themselves with suicidal force. And all could observe the sky slowly flood with rosy reds at dusk.

Rooms at the hotel were always in demand; Pedersen wondered how Ashe had organized a suite on such short notice. Perhaps the hotel made special dispensation for families of the deceased.

On the sixth floor, Ashe answered his knock and extended his hand, barely glancing at the open identification folder. "Detective Pedersen. Good of you to come here." He grimaced. "I'm beat. That's one hell of a ride in after a working day and a long flight." He waved toward an armchair. "Make yourself comfortable. I need to stand a while after all that sitting."

"It is a long drive." Pedersen crossed the room to one of the straight-backed chairs at the round table. Ashe hesitated, then followed and seated himself opposite, his face tight. Nicholas, entering from the bedroom, moved uncertainly to the low armchair.

Roger Ashe had the unequivocal blue gaze of a man who knows his rights. Older now than the man in the photograph, he had aged well. His body was trim and exercised-looking, with no sign of a paunch; only the beginnings of gray touched his temples. The wool suit was handsome, but Pedersen reflected that it would weigh uncomfortably in the warmth of Bay Cove's midday.

"Now," said Ashe, "what can you tell me, sir? You realize my wife—my former wife and I divorced some years ago?"

Pedersen nodded. "And you have remarried. Right now, Mr. Ashe, I think it is you who can tell me some things." Ashe opened his mouth, but Pedersen went on. "We're interested in the time immediately prior to Miss Robinson's death. I believe you spoke with her several times recently." He consulted his notes. "On the twelfth, sixteenth, twentieth and last Friday."

Ashe's eyes widened slightly. "You do your home-work." He paused as though he were reassessing the situation. "Sally and I did speak several times, although I couldn't have recited the dates so . . . nimbly." He smiled. "Our talks concerned a personal matter that had nothing to do with her death."

"What makes you conclude that?"

A knock interrupted them.

"That's room service. I've ordered coffee for us. I could use a stiff drink, but since you're on duty—"

When the door had closed, Pedersen continued. "You were about to tell me how you came to be so sure about what does and doesn't have to do with Miss Robinson's death."

The other man looked confused. "Did I say that? I meant Sally and I talked about something"—his eyes darted toward his son—"purely personal."

The boy's face stiffened.

Not in front of the children, is that it? Pedersen thought. Sorry, sir, we aren't going to be able to respect your sensibilities on that little matter.

"Perhaps," he said, "you should just tell me what brought about that flurry of phone calls and let me judge as to the bearing it has on her death. Did you ordinarily speak so frequently?" And, he added to himself, if you did, what did the new Mrs. Ashe have to say about that?

Ashe sighed. "No. In fact, until recently we hadn't spoken in several months." With an effort, he went on. "I wonder, since the matter was a personal one, if we couldn't talk about it by ourselves, perhaps tomorrow in your office?"

His son turned his face away in an abrupt movement.

"Sorry, Nick, but it was something just between your mother and me. I'd rather . . ."

The young man stood up. "I'll go down to the bar and have a drink. I could use one, too." His face was drawn, his eyes puffy as though he had not slept the night before. "Give me a ring down there, and I'll come up."

"Good." His father walked to the door with him, his arm across the boy's shoulders. "We'll have dinner downstairs after I'm finished with this."

Alone with Pedersen, he said, "I hated to do that, but it was he Sally and I were talking about. Of course he knows that."

Pedersen waited.

Ashe sat down again. He looked strained. "Sal called to tell me about some girl Nick had been seeing. She was upset—the whole thing sounded pretty unsavory." He ran his hand over his mouth in a weary gesture. "I guess Nick never rebelled when he was a kid—the child development people say that's not so good. He's always been such a . . . compliant kid." He seemed to forget Pedersen. "Yet he hated our divorce—that was a bad year. Well." He took a deep breath. "Guess we—I get the rebellion now."

"Did his mother let Nick know she disapproved of this girl?"

"Oh, I think so. I think her disapproval was what it was all about—at first, anyway." His eyes met Pedersen's. "You have kids?"

"A son and a daughter."

"Then you know. The way Nick couched his words suggested that he wanted her to react."

"Couched his words. What did he say?"

"He didn't say, he wrote. He wrote Sally a rather upsetting letter." He flung a nervous glance toward Pedersen. "You didn't come across it? I thought after—in cases like these, the police went through everything, poked through all the personal papers."

"We do have to do that, of course. What did the letter say?"

Ashe's face changed subtly. He was not finding this easy. "The letter just hinted at what had happened, but he seemed to be accusing his mother of . . . not caring about him, prodding him to be normal. Of course, he is normal, perfectly, just shy, but he seemed to be saying something ugly had happened to him and that it was his mother's fault." Again he ran his hand over his face. "Finally, she found out what it was all about. Some woman—he used her services . . ." He seemed unable to go on.

"Services?"

"She was a call girl. Or a sort of call girl—some off-campus variety they have these days. That is, they make themselves available to students. I guess sex on campus is not quite as readily available as some would have us believe. But"—he flushed—"she claimed Nick had given her a social disease." He raised his eyes to Pedersen's. "The whole thing was so distasteful—and so unlikely. Nick, of all people. I doubt that he . . . Nick's a pretty inexperienced boy. Man. Anyway, she was trying to get money from him—not much, a thousand bucks. It was a sort of blackmail, saying she'd tell us all about it if he didn't pay." His face darkened. "Naughty boy, I'll tell Mommy and Daddy and they'll stop paying the bills— that sort of thing. She said she needed the money for treatment." He made a sound of disgust. "Treatment—a thousand bucks. Nick is unsophisticated, but he isn't *stupid*. He thought it was a scam and that she'd ask for more if he paid her once. So he decided to do the telling himself."

"He chose to tell his mother this? Not you?"

"I know. It's crazy—that's why we thought it was . . . well, almost a hostile act toward her. I don't think he's forgiven her for breaking up our marriage." He stopped suddenly. "Good Lord, I must be giving you the impression Nick—"

Pedersen ignored his last remark. "What did you and his mother do? Did you take some action?"

Ashe roused himself. "We—I called Nick and talked with him. Told him to have himself checked over. He said he'd already been to Student Health and they'd given him a clean bill. Then I asked if he was still seeing the woman. He said no, he'd told her he was talking to us about it, and she had suddenly made herself scarce. But he was still uneasy." He frowned. "Kids!"

"Nicholas is not such a kid, Mr. Ashe. He's twenty."

"Twenty is a kid today. Maybe it wasn't for you and me, but we grew up in a different world."

We did indeed, Pedersen thought, twenty today is younger *and* older—mostly, more confused. "When you and Miss Robinson last talked, had she calmed down?"

"Some. She felt a lot of guilt about the whole thing—she's been worried about Nick ever since she and I divorced. Mind you, she had no reason to worry. Nick's done fine—good grades, out for sports, all the ordinary activities."

"Except for girls?"

"He's a little young in that respect, I grant you. The girls like him. In high school he constantly had phone calls and invitations, but he was shy. But no different from a lot of kids his age. Lots of talk, no action." He looked across at Pedersen, his face quizzical. "He got some action."

"That lack of girlfriends was a worry for his mother?"

He stiffened. "Are you suggesting she thought Nick was gay?"

"I'm not suggesting anything."

88

"Just don't. He's a perfectly normal young man, straight as they come. Not that I'd reject him if he weren't—but I'd know. Sally worried that he might have become some sort of misogynist because he hadn't forgiven her for leaving me. There, again I'm making Nick sound like something he isn't. What I'm trying to say is that Nick is okay. He's no woman-hater. He loved his mother. He feels as bad as I do about her death—worse. Suspecting him of having anything to do with her murder would be insane."

"No reason to assume we suspect him of anything. Can you tell me anything else? Did she mention being in touch with her third husband?"

"Carr? Not likely. She'd had a bellyful of him before they split." His tone was sour.

"We have reason to think they were in touch. Did she ordinarily have contact with him? Since she was divorced and moved here, I mean."

His face darkened. "The man lives in Europe. He's not even in the country."

"I see." Pedersen rose and walked across the room to the window and looked out on the darkening scene. He turned back. "Where did you spend Sunday evening?"

"At home with my wife."

"Just the two of you?"

"Our daughter was asleep in her room. We have a two-year-old."

"I see. . . . How long do you plan to stay in town, Mr. Ashe?"

Ashe pushed his chair back and stood. "I've arranged to be here the rest of the week. I want to see that Nick's okay and settled back into school before I leave, and there are other arrangements. She named me as executor."

"Nick is the heir?"

"Yes. I—when will she—the body be available? She wanted cremation."

"You can arrange for it any time you like. Will there be a service?"

"Later, maybe. In Chicago, where she knew people, when Nick can be there."

Pedersen glanced at the window again. It had become a panel of blue-black. Below the starless sky the waves rustled in and out with a soft sucking sound.

"What sort of art did your wife have?" he said.

Ashe started. "Art? Paintings?" He thought. "When we split up she took a couple of prints and a painting done by a friend of hers. She had some posters. She liked posters."

"Sculpture?"

There was a short silence. Then Ashe said warily, "I seem to recall an Eskimo piece. Why? Is something missing?"

"We're not sure. I'll be on my way. Come by tomorrow—you can give Detective Tate a ring and set up a time. I want to talk some more with Nick, and I'll need statements from both of you. Oh, I meant to ask, did you know Miss Robinson's first husband? Creatore?"

Ashe shook his head. His face was drawn with fatigue. "A college romance. She wasn't eighteen when they married. I've never met the man."

As Pedersen turned to leave, Ashe placed a hand on his sleeve. "Thanks for being so decent to Nick yesterday. He told me."

"We're pretty decent people," Pedersen said. "And he's a nice young man."

A nice young man, Pedersen thought as he waited for the elevator, but, he added to himself as the door slid open, did the nice young man murder his mother? Or should he be wondering about Ashe, the self-possessed lawyer, the understanding father, who could not hide the fact that mention of the successor to his former wife's affections still rankled?

90

CHAPTER ELEVEN

"You told him, I suppose."

Ashe had not phoned down to the bar; he had left the suite and joined his son there. Hostility met him.

He countered irritably, "Jesus Christ, Nicky, I don't know how the hell you got yourself into this thing."

Nick was nursing a beer, scowling into it. "You told him, I suppose." His tone was an accusation.

"Of course. I had to—he had the letter." There was a long pause before he spoke again. His weariness had crept into his speech. "How did you ever get involved with this Linda, Nick? I wish I understood you."

"Well, you don't. Mom was bitching all the time about girls, girls, girls—making me feel like some kind of fag. So I'm a little shy, but she didn't know a damned thing about whom I slept with—or whether. Anyway, that's how I got involved. I couldn't very well talk to you about it."

"You couldn't? Why?"

"Because, to put it plainly, you don't give a fuck about me since you have your new family."

"Let's forgo the colorful language. And where exactly did you get the idea I don't care about you?"

"Ha." Nick's laugh was bitter. "Maybe by how much you cared about Mom. How long was it before you married Pam?"

"Nick, what happened between your mother and me was between us. Only. But marrying, and for that matter having another child, has never for one minute made you less important to me. Jesus, Nicky, I love you. You're my *son*."

"How come you can use any language you damned well want to and I can't? Still a little boy, little Nicky. You can start calling me Nick—I asked you to do that a long time ago. In fact, that's what it's all about, if you must know—you and Mom treating me as though I'm still ten years old."

"Look, Nick"—he picked up his drink and stood up —"let's get a table and have this out. For one thing, I need to know everything that happened Sunday night."

"Nothing happened. Not a thing. I said I'd come down and I didn't. That's it. I don't want to talk about it."

"I know how you feel, but even if you had come you might not have been able to prevent—"

"*Please.* I don't want to talk about it."

"I hope you're telling me the truth. If you aren't, you could be in big trouble."

"No more than you."

"How can you say that? I was in Chicago."

"There are planes."

"That's ridiculous. What are you saying?"

"It's been done. Mom told me you planned to come out for some weekend meeting in San Francisco this month."

Ashe's sudden movement splashed his drink on his hand. "I changed my mind about that—and I think it's the better part of wisdom for you to forget about it. I would *not* mention that conference to our Detective Pedersen. Did you hear me?"

They sat glaring at each other in silence until the waiter arrived with the menus.

CHAPTER TWELVE

They spent their evenings at Paul's house.

"Your place or mine?" Eileen had teased that first time, feeling young and excited. And when Paul had seen her house, he had admired the ormolu clock, the Oriental rugs with their warm, faded tones, the deep velvet chairs. "A lady with wonderful taste," he had said. "Wonderful. You should have mentioned that in your ad. 'Superb taste a must!'"

But when she saw his place, the choice was made.

Paul's house was set on a wooded hill, so placed that the deck to the rear sat in the treetops and looked over

94

them to the bay. Inside, the house was full of surprises. Steps led up to one room, down to another. A small indefinable attic room opened off the stairs at the landing; at one end of it, under the peaked roof, an oversized window looked toward the water. The main bedroom was low-ceilinged with dormer windows down its length; some past owner had painted it the color of the sky at noon on a clear day. Eileen had laughed when she saw it. The dining room was a balcony overlooking the living room, and the fireplace reminded her of clay ovens she had seen on a visit to a pueblo in Taos.

And he had collected wonderful treasures: every room offered an object for the eye or hand—a single polished stone, an iridescent shell, a mask from Nigeria, a sturdy little pre-Columbian figure, a cloisonné box, a gnarled bit of driftwood.

She fell instantly and wholly in love with the place.

The house was several miles out of town, and usually they drove out together, Paul picking her up after work. As they sped along the freeway and then bumped up the dirt road to the house, they caught each other up on the day. Tonight, because they had met at the restaurant, she had her own car. "Just as well," she said. "I should get home tonight in case that detective wants to get to me. I'd just as soon he didn't have to ask where I spend my nights."

Paul laughed, an uncomfortable sound. "We could give each other alibis."

At the house, Paul laid a fire, the beginning of their evening ritual. The tray of liqueurs still sat on the coffee table from the evening before, the oversized cushions had not been moved from their place close to the hearth.

But tonight something was wrong between them.

"What is it?" Eileen finally said. Paul had prodded the fire until it stirred into life and had stretched out before it, his head in her lap. For several minutes he had been si-

95

lent, staring into the flames. "Paul? You're miles away. Why are you acting so . . . so . . ."

"I'm not acting any way." He sat up and poured himself another Grand Marnier without offering her one. "I'm uneasy about Zora's talking to that detective. If I were he and heard about something like this, I'd certainly look into it. What exactly did you say to her?"

"I told her not to volunteer anything. After all, as far as she knows, your whole relationship with us consisted of one lunch with me and one with Sally. Afterwards, we agreed the idea had been a poor one, and that was that. There's no reason for her to talk about it."

"There may be no reason, and she may say something anyway."

"She knows better. This is a small town. It may have twenty-five thousand people, but it's a small town all the same."

"That's what worries me. I don't think she'd do anything deliberate, but sometimes things slip out of your control. One news story could have quite an impact on my life. Can't you see the caption? University scientist a suspect in *Happy Times* murder. God!" He sat silent for a few minutes. "You know what I mean. It's like—what? The accident on the highway, I guess. The split second that alters a lifetime."

She sighed. "It would be so unfair if you were to be involved."

"I answered the ad—I needn't have."

"You're scaring me. I know Zora's not going to say anything. You don't report to a detective every dumb idea you've had in the past year."

"Dumb?" He raised his eyebrows.

"Come on, you know I don't mean you. I mean the idea of three women sharing one man." Her head was beginning to ache again.

"Have you found this to be a dumb idea?"

"I just said I hadn't." She picked up her empty glass and then set it down again with care. "Have you?"

"Oh, the original idea was crazy, of course, but something pleasant seems to have come out of it. And I did answer the ad, so it couldn't have been too crazy."

The band of pain around her head was taking hold, tightening. "Is that what our relationship is—something pleasant?"

He laughed. "At the moment, no. But overall, I'd say it's been pleasant. Wouldn't you?"

"Is that all—pleasant?"

"I'm a little old to go into ecstasies. We enjoy each other, we like the sex—"

"And that's it? The sex?"

He reached for the poker and knocked ash off a log. "I keep expecting to hear you say, 'But I'm not that kind of girl.' Is that what you're thinking?"

"No." She stood up, angry. "That's not what I'm thinking. What I'm thinking is that this is just another roll in the hay for you, about what I might have expected from someone who would answer that ad."

"You wrote the ad."

"Damn you," she said. They stood glaring at each other. With an effort, she controlled her voice. "Why are we fighting?" They had quarreled only once before, but the quarrel had been bitter; she knew they were capable of hurting each other.

He took her hands. "Look, Eileen, when we began to see each other, there was no commitment from either of us. I made no promises, you made no promises. We liked what we had—which, incidentally, was not just a roll in the hay. We liked the same things, you enjoyed the house, we liked the same food, the same music—there have been many pleasant—sorry if the word offends you—but *pleasant* aspects to our friendship. Wasn't that enough for you?"

"Past tense? No, of course it's enough. I'm sorry—of course it's enough." She moved away from him and knelt on the cushion. The log suddenly caught and blazed. "You do make good fires." She ran her hand over her forehead. "How are you with aspirin?"

He returned with aspirin and a glass of water. "You take too much of this stuff." He reseated himself on the cushion. "It's this whole business. It's enough to unsettle anyone."

"Paul, we're silly." She swallowed three of the tablets. "Zora doesn't know you—she's barely seen you. There's not a reason in the world—"

He broke in. "That's not precisely so," he said. "She has seen me."

"What do you mean?"

"I mean we met."

Eileen shivered. That drafty window needed fixing; they must have forgotten to draw the curtain. "You met. When did that happen?"

He shrugged, impatient. "Oh, one time. After I'd met you and Sally. She got in touch with me, and I was curious to meet the final member of the mad threesome."

"But you never told me."

"At the time—and now, I might add—I felt under no obligation to tell you whom I saw or did not see." He smiled. "You did request one man for the three of you."

"But it seems in the course of ordinary conversation you'd have mentioned it. And just now to let me go nattering on about how you didn't know her and she didn't know you . . ."

"I have told you. And I can also tell you the meeting was not the most auspicious social occasion of the year."

"What happened?"

"Nothing happened. She just made terribly clear to me that I was not her cup of tea. Not that she's mine, but she didn't trouble to be polite about it."

"That doesn't sound like Zora."

"If you want to know"—his smile was crooked—"I think she had a purpose in meeting me. For some reason, she was deliberately trying to scare me off all of you. Have you ever said anything to her about continuing to see me?"

"No. I don't know why, it was—now don't be angry at the way I put this, but it was as if you belonged to all of us and I was doing something dishonest. I know that sounds ridiculous, but that's the way I felt."

"And you think it was also dishonest of me not to have said something about seeing Zora that once?"

She looked at him, uncertain. "No, not exactly. It does make me wonder what else you haven't told me."

"I said you were running risks, picking up men through ads."

"Men who live in houses buried in the woods? Off dirt roads nobody can ever find?" For some reason, she could not laugh.

"But," she added after a moment, "by the same token, for all you know, I killed Sally Robinson."

"Not likely," he said, and laughed without amusement.

CHAPTER THIRTEEN

Pedersen crept along the two-lane street behind a slow orange school bus, ticking off the items on a mental list—details. He felt marvelous. The call from Freda had set him up. Funny how the whole look of a day was different when he felt like this. He opened the car window.

He had awakened early. With Freda away, mornings were different. It went beyond the silence and the absence of her warm body in bed. The house smelled different. He had become used to the odor of coffee brewing as he shaved, to the mingled scent of toothpaste and cologne when she emerged from the bathroom. The morning paper had no savor without her to exclaim over the news with him. Carrying the newspaper in from the drive that morning, he had realized he even missed her constant interruptions as he read and she struggled with the crossword puzzle. A four-letter word meaning *quagmire* would be a welcome distraction.

Breakfast, too, was flat, routine, a matter only of nutrition. By himself, he stirred instant coffee into hot water from the tap and absently munched a slice of toast and a slab of cheese standing at the kitchen counter. When she was there, breakfasts were a serious matter. Freda was romantic about breakfast. She made the table bright with mats and flowers, wore a crisp-looking housecoat and lipstick, brushed her hair into a becoming nimbus. She served small complicated omelets with chives and cheese and mushrooms or with artichoke hearts and black olives hidden in them.

One morning she had explained. "When I was a teenager," she said, "I read all these articles in the women's magazines on how to keep your man. They all began with breakfast. You put on lipstick, slipped into a starchy little housecoat and baked a batch of baking powder biscuits. If you performed well at breakfast, your husband performed well at night." She laughed. "They didn't quite say that, but the message was clear. I believed every word." Although she had laughed as she told him, and although the only women's magazine he saw her read these days was *Ms.*, he knew she still believed.

He went back to his list. Most of the details were already being dealt with. Dispatch was important. The longer a case dragged on, the less the likelihood of its ever being closed, of the killer being found. Unless a case was bizarre—and some of those remained unsolved or

101

took years to crack—it was most easily broken in the first few days.

An unplanned murder—and he was convinced this had been an unpremeditated act—was most difficult. It was his belief that anyone could kill. The act committed—or averted—depended on provocation, circumstance, opportunity, chance, sometimes a constellation of those that produced the exact climate for crime.

This case, he reflected as he waited for the school bus to pick up a pair of energetic youngsters, did not look as if it were about to fall into place easily. At the moment it was a muddle of impressions.

He thought back over the people who had been a part of Sally Robinson's life. His interviews had been interesting in one particular: in each there seemed an odd contradiction, a discrepancy. Eileen Brande had claimed only casual acquaintance with Robinson, yet had been wary, nervous, evasive. Lou Mullen, so candid in his account of his friendship with Sally, so forthcoming in most respects, had concealed the violence in his past, yet a man as sophisticated as he must have known it would be uncovered with far more sinister implications than if he had mentioned it. The engaging Simone Rabreau, to all appearances not given to jealous vindictiveness and apparently attached to Mullen, had readily revealed her lover's record as a wife-abuser. The missing James Carr had appeared in town quite openly but for unknown reasons and then had mysteriously vanished. And the boy, Nick—was it that letter that disturbed him, or something more? *Your loving son.* The letter's ironic close stayed with Pedersen.

And the father? Was he, as he would have Pedersen believe, firmly ensconced in a new relationship? Why had he reacted so sharply to the notion that Sally might again be in contact with Carr? Or had he already known? This trouble over the boy could have stirred up buried angers,

102

angers in which a moment's rage—but perhaps the old resentments had never ceased. The tightly composed face of Nick's father came back to him, the contained energy, and with it came a recollection of Ashe's tidy attempt at positioning him in a low armchair, while he, Ashe, stood—the sense of masculine vanity, the need to dominate.

The bus he was following turned, interrupting the thought, and Pedersen shot ahead. Zora Hirsch's house was around the next corner. He was curious to meet her. Seeing Sally Robinson's friends in their own settings would tell him not only about them, but also about Sally Robinson. Knowing the people she knew was a step toward knowing her, knowing her life. Understanding her death.

The house, once a Victorian dame of dignified mien, had been what his puritanical father would have called tarted up with pinks and purples. Pedersen had grown up amidst such structures. The whimsy of the new fashions was wasted on him; he liked things in his surroundings to remain predictable. In his work, they seldom did.

Zora Hirsch came to the door with a cigarette in her hand. "I'm thinking of putting up a sign, 'Thank you for not making a fuss over my smoking,'" she said. He wondered how many times she had said those words. "Come in, Detective." Beneath the façade of ease, her clever face was tight, strained.

"I didn't hear till yesterday," she said. "Somehow I got through a whole twenty-four hours without news. Hard to do these days."

Inside, the house looked cool, a little unwelcoming. He had never been taken with rooms furnished in beiges or grays or, as this was, in whites, but he supposed the intent was to show off the handsome rugs; it could do her business no harm to demonstrate what her wares could

103

do for a house. Freda would admire. To him all the chairs looked uncomfortable.

"May I offer you something? Coffee?" She was still being a hostess.

She poured from a handsome Thermos server already set out, and offered him a plate of little crullers.

"Now, Mrs. Hirsch. Tell me about Sally Robinson."

Questions without structure unsettled people. Zora Hirsch immediately became nervous and unsure. "What shall I tell you about her? I mean . . ."

"Whatever you think I should know."

"You're aware that I really didn't know her very well?"

Eileen Brande had said that, too. Why were these women disclaiming knowledge of Sally Robinson? "I had the impression you were one of her closer friends."

"No, no." She gained confidence. "It was a casual acquaintance. I had no *entree* into any of her personal affairs, into any of her secrets." Something in her face told him otherwise.

"Tell me what you do know."

"It's not much. She was a friendly person—light-spirited, I guess you'd say. Optimistic. I think she took life as it came, didn't agonize over things . . ." On her face was that wary expression again.

"Except?"

"Oh . . . maybe a bit over her son. I guess all parents do that. I don't have children myself—perhaps I'm not properly sympathetic."

"What did she worry about in connection with him?"

"Silly things. Why he didn't have a girlfriend, for one." She made a sound of disgust. "He was only twenty."

"Attractive boy?"

"I saw him only once, at a Christmas party. Nice-

104

looking. But it doesn't follow . . ." She left him to guess what didn't follow.

"Tell me about last week."

She looked relieved. "We didn't have our usual lunch."

"When did you see her last?"

"We met a couple of weeks ago."

"Did she talk about her personal life then?"

"Little things, I suppose. Nothing I remember."

"And you've had no contact except in this causal way. Nothing more . . . personal?" He examined her face. "You aren't worrying about keeping some confidence, are you, Mrs. Hirsch? We're looking for a murderer—privacy is no longer important. And you may be assured I'm sharing very little with the newspapers."

Again an expression Pedersen could not decipher crossed her face. "She didn't tell me things in confidence."

"What men was she seeing?"

"She didn't say she was seeing any."

Why did he feel each time she spoke she stopped and chose her words with care? She needed to be thrown off guard.

"Tell me about Sunday night."

"Sunday night." She said it flatly, as though she could make no connection between it and what they were discussing. Then her face changed. "Oh. The night she was . . . died." She stopped to think. "I was by myself. I went to a movie at the Barnhouse—*Lolita*. An old movie I'd seen before." Pedersen made a mental note to see that film next time it showed.

She continued. "I went alone. Some women don't like to go to the movies alone; I never mind." She slid the lid of the inlaid box back again. Pedersen wondered if the interview was doing this to her or if she habitually chain-smoked.

105

"Did you see anyone you know?"

"Nobody I recall." She looked at him with inquiry, obviously waiting for him to name someone she should have seen.

"It's a fairly small theater."

"Yes. But I don't recall seeing anyone I know."

He let it go. "Did Miss Robinson talk about her former husbands at all?"

"One time she told us about them—where she'd met them, their names. I think she and her son's father were in touch. I'm not sure."

"Did you ever see her act?" He was ricocheting among topics, trying to catch her in an unwary moment.

"I usually saw the things she was in. She was good."

"Did you know her friends at the Playhouse?"

"I'd met some—her director and the woman he lives with—or maybe doesn't live with."

"You never met any of her husbands?"

"If they were in town, she didn't introduce them to us."

"You keep saying 'us.'"

"Eileen Brande. The three of us did things together."

"How did you meet?"

"Lord, I don't think I can remember." She crushed her cigarette into an ashtray. "Is that important, too?" Her voice was impatient.

"Have you lived in the town a long time?"

"About three years. I came the year after my husband died. I had been co-owner of a rug shop, and this town looked like a place that could use a shop like that, so I started one here on my own. I'd heard it was a pleasant place to live." Her hand went out for another cigarette, but she checked it.

"Did you find that to be true?"

"Did I find what to be true?"

"That the town needed a shop like yours?"

106

"It's doing quite well."

"And did you find it a pleasant place to live?"

She threw a scornful glance at him and nodded. "Are you the detective in charge of Sally's investigation?" Her tone did not express confidence in him.

"I am." He waited.

"Have you been able to . . . establish what happened to her? It wasn't a break-in?"

"It seems unlikely. Are you familiar with her doors?"

She looked blank. "Her doors?"

"The entrances to her house."

She laughed suddenly. "Oh, that front door. It sticks, you have to know how to open it." She added thoughtfully, "It would be hard for someone who didn't know about that door to get in quietly—is that it?" She smiled. "And the back door is permanently deadbolted. She should have had those fixed long ago. Sally was careless about things like that." She said the last without sympathy.

He looked around the meticulously appointed room. His untidiness had been a sore point with Freda for thirty-two years. Tidy people were not tolerant of those unlike themselves.

"What else will you do?" she asked. "How does a detective track down a murderer?"

"I think if I told you, you'd find it hard to understand. It's not like in the movies; it's slow, dull work."

She studied his face. "Is it useful for other people to . . . help?"

"No. Not only is it not useful, but I think you should know that amateur detectives often become targets themselves. What you can do, though, is tell me what you know."

She was silent.

He considered her. Sally Robinson may have been careless, but Zora Hirsch was not. He had not penetrated her reserve. He hesitated. "Mrs. Hirsch, if there is something you are not telling me, remember that we are trying to apprehend a person who has killed. If he has killed once, he may kill again. Think carefully." He gave her his card.

Her eyes met his. "If I think of anything."

As the door closed behind him, Pedersen swore silently. She was concealing something. Did she know something that made her afraid for her own safety if she told? Or afraid for someone else's? If so, for whose?

Driving back to the station house, Pedersen thought about Sally's companions. Not just with this one but with both, he had a sense of something withheld, information not volunteered. And both, oddly, had claimed little acquaintance with Robinson. Yet Mrs. Nishikawa had spoken of them as Sally's warm friends. It wasn't just those two either, he realized. No one, as he thought about it, was offering anything. Another odd thing. Over and over again, acquaintances spoke of Sally as easy, careless, comfortable. Why should a woman like that produce such a tight-lipped attitude in those around her? Why should she be a problem to others, altogether? He shook his head. Hard to figure what there was in her that could have provoked someone to the fury of that blow.

CHAPTER FOURTEEN

In moments of self-doubt, Pedersen said to his wife that detection was at least seventy-five percent chance and luck. Sometimes one had it; sometimes one didn't. It was such chance that brought him to Paul Shapiro—the mysterious "P." If he hadn't passed the supermarket on his way back to headquarters, if he hadn't decided to pause long enough to look into the matter of steaks, the encounter wouldn't have happened.

He had parked his car and was halfway down the aisle to the meat counter when behind him a shy, somehow familiar voice said his name. He turned to find, barely reaching his chin, the neat dark head of Tamiko Nishikawa tilted toward him. He greeted her with real pleasure. "Mrs. Nishikawa! How nice to see you."

She bobbed her head at him. "I think more," she said. "I think about what you ask. You ask about name of friend?"

His attention focused on her. "Yes. You've thought of something?" Gently, he took her arm and eased her to one side of the aisle, out of traffic.

"Maybe not important. Man, he come sometime? White hair? Name Mr. Shapiro."

Shapiro. Not as bad as Smith, but there could be a couple dozen Shapiros in town, none of them eager to own up to a friendship with Sally Robinson. "Do you remember a first name, Mrs. Nishikawa? It would help me if you could recall it."

She frowned. "Little short name." She gave up and shook her head sadly. "Sorry. I not help."

"You did, you did—you may have helped a great deal. Thank you for your help." He found himself wishing he could bow to her without feeling like an ass.

She bobbed her head several more times, smiling, and then she was gone, scurrying back along the aisle.

He stuck a hand in his pocket and ran the worry beads through his fingers. Now all he had to do was figure out which Shapiro. And why he hadn't come forward.

After a stop at home to assemble and down a sandwich— a sketchy breakfast was not, he had discovered, the best idea; he was starving—he headed back to his office at headquarters.

Before he could make his way down the corridor, Ronald Tate intercepted him. "Carl, hold it."

He slowed. "Ron, I've come up with something. It may be important."

But Tate was not listening. "Carl, guess who's shown up."

110

"Not—?"

"Right. Waiting outside your office. James Freeman Carr the Third."

Pedersen stood before James Carr wondering what being this good-looking did to shape a man. Carr was a striking figure, one to turn heads. Placed alongside him, Nick and Roger Ashe dimmed, became ordinary, physically unworthy of note. Pedersen had read studies of women whose beauty intimidated and defeated men, women who despaired that they were loved only for their faces or bodies, but he could recall no such study concerning handsome men.

As he indicated a chair and settled himself at his desk, he tried to name for himself the qualities that set this man apart. Carr's face was more than aquiline, it had a darkly saturnine cast, yet with the mouth seeming imminently about to express pleasure and the direct, considering gaze, it was a face full of contradictions. The hair receding slightly at the temples merely broadened the brow beneath the graying mane that gave a leonine bulk to the head. As Carr crossed the room to seat himself, his long body was easy. He moved as though he were in tennis shoes crossing a court.

Here was a man women would provoke to turn that confronting gaze on them. Pedersen thought of his own bulk, kept in check only by Freda's continued effort, and his own rough-featured visage, incapable of flirtation or of deception with women, and sighed.

"May I smoke?" Seated, Carr surveyed Pedersen with what could only be amusement. He must be conditioned to appraising stares from those meeting him for the first time.

Pedersen pushed an ashtray toward him. "Mr. Carr," he said, "*where* have you been keeping yourself?"

Carr laughed and then checked himself. "I shouldn't laugh. Nothing about Sally's death is amusing. It's just

111

that you sounded rather like my father used to. I stopped
off en route out of town. My . . . friend and I were staying in a cabin and I had no idea I was wanted. If necessary
I can produce the friend, although"—he gave Pedersen a
glance of complicity—"in the circumstances, I'd rather
not."

"A woman friend?"

Carr nodded.

"It may be necessary. First you'd better begin by telling me what you were doing here. In Bay Cove, I
mean."

Carr drew on his cigarette and lounged back in his
chair. "Well, it's a story. And considering my stopoff on
the way out of town, I may not come out heroically, I
admit. I was here to persuade my former wife to take me
back."

"Take you back. Go to Europe with you? I understand
you live in Paris."

"Not exactly. I mean I do live in Paris, but I wasn't
asking her to come there. What I wanted was for her
to"—he had difficulty in wording it—"let me be with her
while I was here in the country."

"Rather like an inexpensive bed-and-breakfast?"

Carr's face darkened, and he flung an angry look at
Pedersen. "I suppose you assume I deserve that."

"I suppose I do."

"It wasn't like that. Not at all. I'm—I was honestly
fond of Sally. I always have been. I think it's appalling,
what's happened to her."

"When you finally heard what did happen to her, how
did you account for it?"

"You mean do I have any idea who killed her?"

"That's the idea."

Carr shrugged. "I have absolutely no answers. The
whole thing is incredible to me. Sally was a warm, generous woman with not a malicious bone in her body. I
can't imagine anyone's even thinking of hurting her."

"Murdering her."

Carr flinched. "Yes."

"Suppose you tell me exactly what happened on Sunday. I assume you were with her then—and when else? When did you get into town?"

"I drove down Friday night—came into San Francisco Airport and rented a car. We'd already talked several times—while I was in Paris and here—and we had the thing pretty much settled by then. I checked into a bed-and-breakfast here . . ." He flushed again. "I didn't want to rush her till we'd met and . . . firmed things up."

God, Pedersen thought, the man sounds as though he's discussing a business deal. He tried to keep his distaste from his face.

"At any rate, we talked on the phone for a long time Friday night and made plans for dinner the next day. She had a rehearsal in the morning and had already made lunch plans. I guess I didn't give her much notice as to when I was coming."

Pedersen did not comment.

Carr went on. "So. We had drinks at her place and then dinner at the Glade—nice restaurant for a little town—and went back to her house."

"You stayed over?"

"Yes. We slept late"—his gesture spoke for him—"and had brunch. Sally is—was a good cook. We talked some more, sort of getting things straight about our plans, and she made us something to eat around three. Then I left. I had my things at the bed-and-breakfast and some work to do, and I wanted to get away early the next morning. I had intended to go right back East to finish up some business, but when I got to San Francisco I made a phone call and found they weren't ready for me. So I made another call and was . . . waylaid."

Laid is the operative part of that word, Pedersen commented to himself. What a cold bastard this was. "Why,

113

if you had this . . . connection in San Francisco, did you need Sally Robinson?"

Carr bridled. "I resent your tone, Detective, and your question. I did not *need* Sally. I wanted to resume our relationship. I have always wanted to—since our divorce."

"And you say you worked all this out by mail?" There had been no recent letters from Carr among those in the shoebox.

"Phone. I don't write many letters. Terrible correspondent." He smiled with self-indulgent tolerance at his shortcoming. Apparently, his pique had passed.

"Did you plan to remarry? You and Miss Robinson?"

Alarm crossed his face. "Oh, I don't think so. We didn't talk about it."

"What about all the time you spend abroad? A little hard to sustain a relationship when you're apart the larger portion of the time." Freda crossed his mind.

"That's true. It would have been hard in that sense."

You'd have suffered, I'm sure, thought Pedersen.

"She could have come over, but she was all wrapped up in some theater group, and she seemed to like the part-time aspect of it. To be honest, so did I. A full-time relationship can be oppressive."

Part-time with you would be too much for some of us, Pedersen reflected.

As though he were aware of Pedersen's thoughts, Carr smiled and leaned forward. The smile was engaging; that was inescapable. "You think I'm a real bastard, don't you, bedding two women in a few days this way? It's just not so. I felt a genuine affection for Sally. She's the only woman I ever wanted to marry and I was sorry things didn't work out for us. This other woman—girl, really—doesn't mean a thing. I made a phone call and discovered I could stay over a couple of days, so I drove to Mill Valley. She has a place—very secluded, as you can imag-

114

ine; otherwise I'd have heard about Sally sooner. I just dropped in to write *finis* to our friendship. I told her what I was planning for the future."

"And she let you stay?"

"She's a very . . . mellow lady. Also I didn't mention it till the day I left."

The man was totally amoral. "At precisely what time did you leave Miss Robinson?"

"Precisely? I don't know that I can say that. Right after we ate, though—early. Four-ish."

"Did she speak of any plans she had for the evening?"

"I had the impression she was going to curl up with a book or something. I don't think she had plans."

"Any phone calls while you were there?"

"Well, actually, she unplugged the phone Saturday night. She said her director had a way of calling at odd hours and she didn't want to be . . . interrupted. We forgot all about plugging it back till Sunday afternoon. No calls after that."

"Did she talk to you about anyone here, give you any idea she was worried about anything, involved in anything that could have been troublesome?"

"Absolutely not. She seemed on top of the world. Relaxed. Happy. Back in Chicago, when we were together, I know she had some questions about me, but somehow they didn't seem to matter much anymore. She talked about how much she enjoyed her friends here and her theater group and how much she liked the freedom of not being married. She was a little worried over Nick, her son, but she'd worried over him ever since she divorced his father. Worrying is the thing mothers do best."

"Nick lived with you and Miss Robinson?"

"God, no, he couldn't stand the sight of me. He stayed with his dad. Roger is a decent chap—and a good father, or so Sally thought. She felt guilty about the breakup, so she worried about Nick."

115

"One further question. You're an art dealer. You must have been aware of what your wife had by way of art in her home. You may have given her some of it. Can you tell us what she had—prints, paintings, sculpture?"

Carr frowned. "She didn't have much. Several framed posters—some I gave her, a Munch, a Pissarro, a couple of old Galerie Maeght things I had around—a Miró and a Kandinsky, I think. She had a Baskin print and a Peterdi—she'd had those forever. The only painting I can think of was done by a friend of hers—I'm afraid you'll never find it in the annals. She had a piece of Eskimo sculpture I brought back from a buying trip in Toronto, and I sent her a poster from the Beaubourg—the Pompidou in Paris, you know—that Paris '37/'57 show they did. I think that's it."

Pedersen wondered if he looked as though he knew what the man was talking about. Freda might. Maybe, he reflected wryly, he'd spent too much of his time in college on psychology courses.

"That's all? No other sculpture, nothing like that?"

"I can't think of anything. What's missing?"

"If you do, let me know. We'll need a statement from you—Detective Tate will take that. And I want you to keep me informed as to where you are. How long will you be in town?"

"I have a reservation for a Friday flight. I guess I'll just stay on here till then. I find I'm more shaken up than I thought. Here's where I'll be." He scrawled a name on a business card.

"One more thing. If anything—anything at all—comes to mind, anything she said or you noticed, I want you to call me. Even if it seems unimportant. If I'm not here, leave a message with Detective Tate."

Carr rose. "I will, I promise you." He extended his hand. For the first time an expression of pain crossed his face. "Get the man who did this, Detective. Get the bastard."

116

Pedersen sat looking at the door that had closed behind Carr. The touch of melodrama at the end bothered him. Was the man, like his former wife, merely a good actor? Had that last moment been the obligatory expression of grief, or had it been genuine, felt? Or was he, as a man so unconcerned with morality might be, one of the world's engaging psychopaths? Hard to believe he could have murdered Sally Robinson and then presented himself with such ease, smoothness. But of course smoothness was the trademark of the psychopath. Pedersen shook his head and rang Tate's extension.

Tate grinned as he entered. "One good-looking bastard, isn't he?"

"Bastard is right. I must be old-fashioned."

"You are."

"So be it. Get a signed statement. Then make a note to check Carr's girlfriend—he'll tell you about her. Ask her how Carr seemed when he arrived at her place. He's a very smooth cookie."

"You think. . . ?"

"I just don't know. What happened with the call to Creatore?"

"We can forget him. He hasn't seen her in years. Never been to Bay Cove. Didn't know anything about her third marriage."

"Anything he could tell you that seemed pertinent?"

"Same thing we've been hearing from everybody. Even ex-husbands love her. Warm, easy, comfortable to be with, amusing, all the same things everyone else has said about her."

"Careless?"

"Careless? I don't think he used that word. Why?"

"It's the other word people use to describe her. Probably unimportant. And you confirmed that what he was saying was on the up and up?"

"All okay. No way he could have gotten here and

117

back, no way. He sounded upset that she'd been killed. Said he couldn't imagine—"

"I know, how anyone could want to kill her. Nobody can. Hell, maybe it's our mistake. Maybe the woman wasn't murdered at all."

Tate looked disapproving.

"All right. Did that check turn up anything criminal in the pasts of our people?"

"It's in that folder in front of you. Mullen, the assault, suspended sentence. Nicholas Ashe, misdemeanor, drunk and disorderly, resisting arrest. Ended up with a night in jail and a fine. Carr, speeding, several times. Had his license suspended for a year back in the seventies. Hirsch had a moving violation, too."

Pedersen shook his head.

Tate laughed. "It seems a little excessive—I was surprised we didn't find Mrs. Nishikawa had held up a gas station."

Pedersen smiled. "While we're looking into the criminal element in our midst, we might as well check out Nick's girlfriend, too—put the fear of God into her. Maybe she'll stop her penny-ante blackmailing." He paused. "Now then. I've come up with a new name— one we haven't come across before: Shapiro." He explained. "When you've finished with Carr, let's look into it."

"No such name in her address book," said Tate, checking.

The telephone directory yielded up eleven Shapiros. None had a given name beginning with P. The published City Directory offered nothing additional.

"How about the university directory?" Tate said. "Robinson worked on campus part-time—maybe she met someone up there."

They found one Shapiro, initials R.P., a scientist. "What do you think?" Tate asked.

"She was in Admissions, nothing to do with the sciences, but let's try them all."

Tate added the name to his list.

"Visit, I think, not phone," Pedersen said. "Leave the scientist till last. Start on the others."

With white hair as the identifying feature, Tate tackled the list. The first Shapiro with anything resembling white hair, what was left of it, was in his late eighties; by no stretch of his imagination could Tate couple the man with the young-spirited Sally. Four, tracked down at work, were dark-haired, too young. One was, a neighbor reported, on a month-long honeymoon in Hawaii. The rest could not be found at home. None of those with whom Tate spoke had ever met Sally Robinson.

In mid-afternoon, Tate, who was beginning to develop an aversion to the name Shapiro, phoned Pedersen. "Five to go. Six with the scientist. I'm not finding these guys home—I'd save a lot of time by waiting till evening."

"Makes sense. It's nearly three. You knock off for a while. I'll take on the scientist—hope he's still around at this hour. Call me back around five, just in case this is our man."

The scientist was not still around. By the time Pedersen had discovered that his office was not on campus but in the marine biological laboratories building itself, and he had driven down to the bay, the man had left for the day. Nonetheless, when Tate phoned at five he could pick up the elation in Pedersen's voice.

"White hair," Pedersen said. "In his fifties. Lives in the hills south of town—all they had at the lab office was a box number."

"What's his name?" Tate asked.

"Reuben Paul Shapiro. Known in the labs as Paul."

"Our man." At either end of the line a man grinned.

CHAPTER FIFTEEN

The phone was ringing. Zora struggled to slide the key into the lock without dumping the grocery bag and smashing two dozen eggs.

She made it to the phone before the ringing ceased.

"I got you at a bad time."

"Eileen. Let me set this bag down and get my breath." She pulled off her sweater and returned to the phone. "What's up?"

"I just wanted to talk for a minute. Have you time?"

Zora sat down before the telephone. "I have to get over to the shop in a few minutes."

"I'll be quick. Did that detective come to see you?"

"About an hour ago. I dashed out to the store right after he left. I didn't say anything about our ad."

"Good—I'm glad. Paul is one of the things I wanted to talk about."

"Paul?"

"Paul Shapiro. I've been seeing him, Zora. He told me about your meeting."

"Not much to tell. We met just once—I was curious."

"He said you weren't very encouraging. He thought you might be trying to scare him off all of us."

Zora laughed. "Maybe I was, without knowing it. The whole thing made me uneasy, especially knowing both you and Sally were seeing him. I did know."

There was a silence.

Zora spoke. "Did I say something I shouldn't have? You must have guessed he was seeing Sally?"

"Actually, I didn't. She never mentioned it."

"Did you mention to her that you were seeing him?"

"No. But then, we've barely seen each other these last few weeks."

"Well?"

After a moment, Eileen said, "You think I—we're wrong about him?"

"Wrong? What do you mean?"

"Just . . . I've been accepting him as I would any other man—honest, trustworthy man. Maybe he's something else altogether."

Zora considered. "Did you have an agreement that you wouldn't see anyone else?"

"No, nothing like that. It's just that he never said one word about you or Sally. Wouldn't you think he'd have mentioned it?"

"Not if he was looking us all over to see whether one of us appealed to him."

"It stands everything on its head. It—scares me."

121

"Because of Sally's death?"

"No. I don't know." Anxiety permeated her words.

"Does Paul seem threatening?"

"You mean do I think he'll pick something up and bash me?" She laughed uncomfortably. "Obviously, I don't think that. Do you think he would?"

"I don't know the man."

"You sound funny. You are suspicious."

"Eileen, I don't know the man. Christ!"

"What are you swearing at me for? You are uneasy about him. I—I just hate to tell that detective about him. If he's perfectly innocent, he won't seem that way, answering our ad, seeing all of us, the whole business."

Zora was silent.

"Zora?"

"Have you talked to him at all about Sally's death?"

"A little. He didn't like the idea of our mentioning him to the police. Naturally."

"Understandable."

"It's just that it seems . . ."

"Seems what? I do wish you'd finish a sentence now and then, Eileen."

"Don't bark at me. There's no point in our being angry with each other. Right now, we need each other."

Zora sighed. "I'm sorry. The whole business has unstrung me. You, too, I'm sure."

"What did Paul say about Sally?"

"He didn't say much about either of you—that would hardly have been appropriate while he was having lunch with me. All he said was that he thought she played the field. And that she was comfortable to be with. No one ever talks about how comfortable I am to be with."

"Nor me."

"Look, Eileen, I've got to put my groceries away. Let's just keep quiet about the ad. For our own sakes, I'd just as soon it wasn't known."

"It was a stupid thing to do, wasn't it, advertising? What possessed us, do you think?"

"Who knows? It wasn't smart."

"Yet . . ."

Zora glanced at the bag of groceries. "Everything else okay?"

"I guess. Lunch soon?"

"Maybe next week. But keep in touch. I mean that— let me know what's going on."

As she transferred the carton of eggs and the container of milk from the brown paper bag to the refrigerator, she thought, Should I? Would that be the safer thing to do, to tell the police about the ad? A number of emotions were at odds in her; it was hard to sort them out. In the end they all came down to fear and conscience, she supposed. Fear said, tell them. Conscience said, you can't know— think of the damage you might do. She could hear her father saying, "It's not just a cliché, Zora. Conscience is the most reliable guide. Do what your conscience says is right."

CHAPTER SIXTEEN

"Nick. All alone? May I come in?"

In the doorway stood Jim Carr, tall, self-possessed, the same hated figure he had been during all the years of his mother's marriage. With an effort, Nick stood aside.

Carr stepped into the room and turned. "You're alone?"

Unable to speak, Nick nodded.

"Good." He crossed to a chair near the window. "Sit down, Nick. I want to talk for a minute."

Dumbly, Nick took a chair.

"First I want to say how sorry I am. I know this must

be hard for you. For me, too. Did your mother tell you we had—found our way to a reconciliation?"

Nick mumbled a word.

"Was that yes? Listen, fellow, I know you've never cared for me, but surely you wanted what was right for your mother—you loved her."

Nick stared at him wordlessly.

"All right." Carr became impatient. "You don't have to talk to me. I really wanted to check out something else with you." He approached his subject warily. "I thought—did I see you Sunday night? I thought I did."

Nick could hear that his own voice sounded wrong, choked, as though he were forcing the words through his throat. "At my mother's."

"I thought so. I—" The sound of a key in the lock interrupted his words. For a moment Roger Ashe stood framed in the door, staring at the two.

"Carr."

Jim Carr rose from his chair. "Roger. I came by to say how sorry I am."

"Decent of you." The voice was without warmth.

"Not a matter of being decent. I was just telling Nick that Sally and I'd had a reconciliation. This is more of a loss for me than for you."

"Perhaps *I* should have visited *you*." Nick watched his father, with an effort, control himself. "It's a loss for everyone." Roger Ashe's tone had become deliberately neutral.

"Actually, I came by to see Nick, not you. He's the one who's going to feel this most."

"I'm aware of that."

There was an uncomfortable silence. "I . . ." each of the two older men said, and stopped.

In a moment Nick's father spoke. "A reconciliation. What sort of reconciliation was that? Sally wasn't going to Paris, was she?"

"No, no, she wanted to stay here. It was—we were planning to see each other as often as we could. Here. I fly in several times a year, some months as often as twice." After a pause he added, "You, I understand, are now the father of a young daughter."

"I am, but"—his tone was aggressive—"that doesn't make Nick's welfare of less concern to me. Nor was Sally's. We always remained in touch. Especially lately."

Carr raised his eyebrows. "Lately?"

"A family concern." Nick knew the dismissive tone well. "Nothing you need to worry about."

"But I do worry. Sally told me Nick had been in some sort of trouble."

Involuntarily, Nick spoke. "She told *you*?"

"She had no business," his father said hotly. "That's Nick's affair, not yours. If there was anything to be done, you're the last person Nick would turn to. Damn Sally, she never had any discretion."

"I'm aware that you always considered me one of her indiscretions—or instances of bad judgment, but that doesn't alter the fact that she had confidence enough in me to—share things with me."

"*Share* things." The tone was mocking. "Is that what she did? I'm not so sure it was confidence she was expressing—Sally just never could handle anxiety without involving everyone she knew."

"I'd hardly say I was just someone she knew. And really, Roger"—the voice had become infuriatingly patronizing—"I don't think you need explain Sally to me. I—"

Nick moved suddenly.

Jim Carr began again. "Are—will you be having a service here?" He spoke to Nick.

His father answered for him. "No. Later there'll be a memorial service in Chicago where she had friends."

"I'd like to come."

"If you're in the country," his father said shortly.

"I'll make a point of it. Nick, I'll give you my address. You let me know."

Nick remained silent.

"How's school been going? Everything all right?"

"Yes."

"Chosen your major?"

"Yes."

Carr spoke with urgency. "Look, Nick, I know I'm not your favorite person, but I care that your mother is dead, just as you do. Freezing me out doesn't change that."

Nick shook his head slowly, still not meeting Carr's eyes. "I'm not freezing you out. I have nothing to say to you." His voice was all right now. He lifted his eyes. With intensity he said, "We have nothing to say to each other. Not *anything*."

Something beyond words passed between them. Carr nodded. "No, I guess not. I guess not," he said.

As he moved toward the door, Nick experienced a moment of pure pleasure as he heard defeat in the voice of the man who had been his mother's husband.

CHAPTER SEVENTEEN

The Richards Marine Biological Laboratories looked different on an ordinary weekday. Earlier, Pedersen had visited as part of a group on a University Open House Day, when the Farm, the Garden, the Labs all were on view to the community. He had liked lingering in the long corridors lined with trays of marine creatures moving about in shallow waters among the rocks and algae. Underseascapes had a magnetic quality—he was drawn into the tiny, vibrantly colorful, delicate world with its unlikely creatures. He became a child again, all disbelief suspended, as he gazed at their eerie transparency, their flowery undulations.

The undersea life on exhibit bore no relation to Paul Shapiro's office. Not so much as a seashell cluttered his desk and the white-haired man who sat behind it studying a report might have been any corporate executive, any professor reading a student thesis.

Pedersen tapped on the open door. "Dr. Shapiro?"

The other man put down the paper and nodded.

"Can you spare a few minutes?" Gently, he nudged the door behind him shut. "I'd like to talk to you about Sally Robinson. Detective Sergeant Pedersen."

Paul Shapiro tossed a nervous glance past Pedersen. "Let's—there's a place outside." Without ceremony, he hustled them through the double doors of the building, down the walk and out of earshot.

The morning was brilliant with sunlight; no summer fog to burn off, not even a chill in the air. They moved toward the bay, not speaking. Then Pedersen said, "Nothing to be alarmed about—I just want to chat for a few minutes. We're wondering why, since you were one of the last to see Sally Robinson alive, you didn't come forward to tell us what you knew of her."

Shapiro frowned. "Isn't it obvious? I didn't have anything to tell, and I wanted to spare myself—and those two women—the embarrassment. It's not as though I knew anything that would help."

"Those *two* women?"

"Come, Detective, you're here because one of them has told you about me—about the ad."

"No."

Shapiro laughed. It was not a pleasant sound. "All right, I'll go along. I answered an ad in *Happy Times*—three women advertising for an escort."

129

"Three women. Who were they?" He was sure he knew.

"I suspect you know. Sally, Zora Hirsch, Eileen Brande."

"I see." Pedersen was quiet for a while, staring off toward the gulls dipping and looping above the water. "You're mistaken, Dr. Shapiro. No one else has confided this information. Tell me, did you become an escort to them?"

"Jesus, you make me sound like a gigolo. No, I did *not* become an escort to them."

"Could you tell me what took place Saturday between you and Sally Robinson?"

"Nothing world-shaking, I assure you. All that happened is that I explained to her that I thought I should stop seeing her. Our relationship was slight, anyway, but I wanted no confusion. I have"—his face twisted—"had become attached to someone else, seriously attached."

"One of the other two."

"Yes. Eileen Brande. The lady who, I assume, turned me in to you."

Pedersen ignored that. "What was Miss Robinson's reaction to your announcement?"

"She laughed. It seems she had also made another commitment."

"You parted on good terms?"

"Not only that. She seemed happy, pleased with her plans."

"Did she say what they were—to whom she had this commitment?"

"Yes. She was resuming a relationship—part-time, it sounded like, since he lives abroad—with her former husband, the one she divorced a few years back. The art dealer."

"You saw all three of the women?"

130

"I met them. One—Mrs. Hirsch—I saw just once. The other two I saw fairly regularly."

"You had a sexual relationship with both?"

"My God, sex and violence—is that what we're getting at? I really don't think I have to answer a question like that."

"We think she was killed by someone she knew."

Shapiro snorted. "Well, it wasn't me. I. She was a pleasant woman, easy to be with, pretty, cheerful, but she never inspired any strong emotions in me—positive or negative. I'm sure she had other—friends." He paused, his face unreadable. "Her death made me sad, of course—murder is always shocking."

"It is—and too common." He was quiet for a moment. "Now then, Dr. Shapiro, you work for the laboratories as a marine biologist. Where do you live?"

The scientist gave his box number. "No street address—I'm off the beaten track. My place is in the hills southeast of town on a little dirt road—Pheasant Trail. Off that."

Pedersen looked at the other man with interest. "You must have a time getting in to work. The commute's heavy from that area."

"I've found a way of cutting through without using the freeway. It's longer, but there's no traffic."

"So you can make it in—what, a half hour?"

"Almost. About thirty-five minutes. I did *not* make the trip into town Sunday."

Pedersen nodded. "What were you doing Sunday night?"

Shapiro thought for a moment. "I was home. Yes. Yes, Eileen had planned to come up for dinner, but she'd worked in her garden all afternoon and was bushed, so she begged off. I read and listened to some music. Then I

131

switched on the news for a few minutes and turned in. Would have been eleven-fifteen, eleven-thirty."

"You didn't speak to Sally Robinson or see her on Sunday?"

"Sally? No, I told you, I didn't expect to see her again. At all."

"Did Mrs. Brande know you were seeing Sally Robinson?"

Shapiro looked away. "I never told her. I have an idea she knows now."

"Why do you think that?"

The scientist looked at him for a moment without speaking. Then he said, "Because you're here."

Pedersen regarded him thoughtfully. "What's your marital status right now, Dr. Shapiro?"

"I'm divorced. Amicably. My wife—former wife—is in the East." He frowned. "You're sure this is just a brief chat?"

Pedersen laughed. "Not much more, just this. Was there anything in Sally Robinson's life that in your mind connects with her murder—anything bothering her, anything odd?"

"The oddest thing I know of was that crazy ad of theirs, but that was back last summer. Maybe she connected with someone else who answered."

"Did she ever speak of doing that?"

He shook his head. "She never spoke about it at all after the first time we met. I think the subject made her uncomfortable. Anyway, I don't suppose she'd have chosen me to tell."

"No, I suppose not. Well, I guess that's it." Pedersen turned to hand him a card. "If you think of anything, use this. Thank you for your cooperation."

Motive, Pedersen thought, as he backed his car out of the parking space. No motive that he could see. The relationship's end was mutually desired. Shapiro's story had

the ring of truth, though he could have been more attached to the woman than he was saying, they could have
quarreled. Shapiro seemed the scientist, cool and reason-
able to his fingertips, hardly impulsive or violent, even
when angry. But Pedersen had seen too many cool crimi-
nals to be misled by a surface. Odd, too, that Shapiro had
suspected Eileen Brande of, as he put it, turning him in—
especially odd if they were lovers. He would have to talk
to her, to both of the women, in fact, to see whether they
bore out Shapiro's story.

CHAPTER EIGHTEEN

Nick Ashe sat before Pedersen, his face tense. "You must know why I didn't tell you. You'd have thought—well, what you're thinking now."

"Why did you turn back to Berkeley—and how far into town had you got before you turned back?"

"All the way. Once you hit the hill, there's not much place to turn off before Bay Cove. I came in, but by then, I knew I didn't want to talk to her, so I circled around and headed back."

"Without a pause?"

Nick dropped his eyes. "I stopped for coffee. I wanted to think it over."

"Tell me from the beginning. What were you going to talk with her about?"

"All kinds of things." He raised his eyes to Pedersen's. "Her attitude toward me."

"What did you plan to say about it?"

The boy was slowly tearing a matchbook to bits, dropping scraps into the ashtray on Pedersen's desk. "I was going to tell her that if she didn't get off my case, I didn't want to see her anymore. At all." He raised his chin, defiant.

"Could you have done that?"

The boy picked up the metal ashtray and cracked it back down on the table. "If I'd had to. Every time I went there, it was like being in a box."

"A box?"

"It was like I was shut off from her—there was no way to get out, to get to her. Ever since Carr. I felt that way then, too. That empty. . . You know what he always reminded me of? Those dummies—mannequins—you see in the windows of men's stores. Made of plastic or composition, hollow, with those perfect"—he rummaged for the word—"*puerile* faces, no expression. Or maybe a sort of all-purpose expression. That must have been just what he looked like when he was younger, you know, like one of those dummies. Now"—his face twisted—"he has a few becoming streaks of white hair. But no more substance."

"Did he have streaks of white in his hair when you last stayed with them?"

"Maybe not. No. He does now."

"How do you know?"

"I—" The boy stopped.

"You saw him last weekend."

135

"I—actually, I—" He could not say it.

"Again. What happened when you came to town Sunday?"

Nick gave a little involuntary shudder and sat forward in his chair. "All right. This is the truth—all of it, this time. I didn't even tell my father this. I did have a cup of coffee and I was going back, then I thought, well, why not circle past the house? If I saw she was in, maybe I'd stop. So I did that. There was a car I didn't know parked in the driveway, so I figured one of her women friends was there, and I was going to go on by. Then just as I'd almost reached the house, the door opened and Jim Carr came out."

"You just caught a glimpse of him?"

"No, I saw him. It was Carr all right. But I was curious. I swung around the block and followed his car—it was just taking off as I got back to the house. He drove to some bed-and-breakfast place, and I had a good look at him when he got out. He was just the same. A little older, with some white in his hair, but just the same. The way he walks . . . Then I did take off for Berkeley."

"You didn't call your mother or stop at the house?"

"No. I just went home. I thought of going back to remind her of a few things, but I didn't."

"What things were those?"

"Oh. Just how boring she found all Jim Carr's posturing after a while. He isn't stupid, but he spends a lot of time impressing people with how handsome he is, how wonderful. He also likes other women to admire him. I don't think my mother appreciated that. They had a lot of fights at the end."

"What time did you get to Bay Cove? And when did you leave?"

"I got in about five-thirty. Quarter of six, maybe. I couldn't have been here an hour."

"Did your mother come to the door to see Carr off?"

136

"If she did, I didn't see her. I was concentrating on him."

"Did he wave, turn to say goodbye, anything of that sort?"

"No. He just came out and headed straight for the car."

Pedersen rose. "All right, Nick. I want you to give Detective Tate all this, exactly as you remember it."

The boy continued to sit in his chair. "Detective Pedersen, my lying—is this—do you suspect me now? Because I didn't do anything to my mother. I couldn't have. I loved her." He gestured in an odd little motion. "You can see—I couldn't even bring myself to talk to her . . ."

After he had gone, Pedersen picked up the ashtray and looked at the bits of paper.

The time conflicted with that in Carr's account. If Nick was telling the truth, Carr must have left Sally around six-thirty, even seven. Surely, the coroner wasn't off by that much; his estimate of the time of death had been between nine and midnight. He recalled once, early in his work in the department, Rand's saying to him, "It's a guess, Carl, an informed guess. We can never be sure by more than twelve hours." Could Carr have left Sally Robinson dead at six-thirty? At seven?

Odd that the boy had not mentioned that possibility. He had never been told the time of death, yet he had not expressed a whisper of suspicion of the man he so disliked.

He was still at his desk, rolling the worry beads between his fingers and thinking of his two encounters of the morning, when the phone buzzed. He spoke into the box. In a few minutes he rang the switchboard. "Put Mr. Mullen on."

"I've thought of something, Pedersen—uh, Officer," Mullen said. "If you need to check my alibi, ask that rug-

137

shop woman. She saw me. I was out getting popcorn and I had to climb over her. She'll remember."

"Thank you." Pedersen rang off. Popcorn? But you got to the Barnhouse late, Mullen—Simone told me. What were you doing buying popcorn and missing still more of a movie you are so enthusiastic about? There was something strange here. What was Mullen's big concern over establishing an "alibi"?

When he had talked to Zora Hirsch, she said nothing about Mullen; in fact, she specifically stated that she had seen no one she knew. Perhaps Mullen had just come in, not gone out to buy popcorn. If he had come in at nine-thirty, or even nine, he could easily have made a stop en route, a stop at a house only blocks from the theater. He must have seen Hirsch in the audience and hoped she had seen him. Better double-check with her, nudge her memory to see if Mullen surfaced, get those times straight.

But when Pedersen reached her, Zora Hirsch had no recollection at all of seeing Mullen.

"And did the women bear out Shapiro's story?" Tate asked, over lunch.

"They did. I got to them right away—I don't think Shapiro had reached either of them. They were pretty uncomfortable about the whole thing and very interested in how I knew about him—I didn't tell them—but they didn't argue about the facts. Brande has been seeing him. Hirsch hadn't told us about Shapiro because Brande asked her not to—and Brande hadn't told us because she couldn't decide whether she should be defending him or avoiding him." He shook his head. "*You* aren't planning to advertise, are you, Ron?" Ronald Tate and his wife had separated earlier in the year.

Tate smiled. "Advertise? At the moment, I wouldn't

take on anyone if she offered herself with a bonus Porsche thrown in. I'm not in the market."

Pedersen laughed. "You're sure—a Porsche?" He sobered. "Give yourself time. Give yourself time, Ron."

"I know. That's what they all tell me. Time does it." He sighed. "I suppose everyone can't be wrong."

CHAPTER NINETEEN

Despite the boy's piteous appeal, he was now clearly in the running, Pedersen reflected as he pulled away from the restaurant where they had lunched and headed for the supermarket. As was Carr. And Mullen's position seemed to grow shakier with each day. Shapiro, for the moment at least, was an unknown quantity as the only other man to have recently had a close—how close was unclear—relationship with the victim. As Pedersen pulled into the supermarket parking lot, he decided he didn't like it. It was a case too cluttered with suspects having means and opportunity, and not nearly cluttered enough with suspects having motives.

He made one stop at the liquor store for wine and headed home. Everything stowed away, he gave a last look around the house. The previous evening he had vacuumed, changed the bed, washed the dirty coffee cups that had somehow strewn themselves about the house. That morning he had bought flowers. Freda wasn't taken in, ever; she would know that this was the first day of her absence in which he had achieved a degree of normalcy in the house. But it would please her that he had made the gesture.

He picked up a couple of the packets of peanuts he kept in a drawer in the kitchen—by now, it seemed a while since lunch—and dropped them into his pocket. Behind him, he closed and locked the door, leaving lights on inside so the house would welcome Freda when she arrived; then he was on his way back to headquarters.

In his office he found a message. No name; merely a phone number. *Call back when convenient.*

He rang the number. No answer. He'd try again in a while. Opening the folder Tate had left him, he spread its contents on his desk.

A half hour later he roused himself from his reading and picked up the phone again. This time the call was answered. At the other end, the voice of James Carr spoke to him. "Detective Pedersen. Oh, good. Glad you called; I wanted to tell you something. I realize I misinformed you. I said I left Sally around four on Sunday. On thinking it over, I realize it was later—more like six-thirty or seven. Unimportant, but I want to be accurate. I must have been pretty shaken when I talked with you."

Alone in his office, Pedersen raised his eyebrows. Shaken. Hardly. You just wanted to distance yourself from the evening on which you knew Sally was murdered.

"In fact," the other man went on, and as he talked Pedersen calculated. Carr must have realized that Nick Ashe would tell him when it was that he had seen Carr coming from Sally's house. He was covering himself, trying to avoid any accusation of lying. Then Pedersen's distracting thoughts were penetrated by what Carr was saying. "What?" he said. He sat up. "Would you repeat that?"

Carr repeated it.

CHAPTER TWENTY

"Chilly out there." Twenty minutes late, breathless, Eileen slid into the booth.

"We can't keep meeting like this," Zora remarked dryly. "You're late. Why the S.O.S? I thought I said yesterday this wasn't a good week for lunch."

"I know. I was upset."

"Anyway, I've shelved everything for a couple of hours. What are you upset about?"

"What do you think?" She studied the menu and then slapped it down on the table. "Let's get the waitress off our backs. Soup and salad?"

"And wine." They ordered. "Now, what's bothering you?"

"What's bothering me is your telling Pedersen."

"My telling Pedersen what?"

"About Paul. What else?"

"*My* telling him! *I* didn't tell him—I thought you did. He just came by to find out if it was true about our meeting Paul through the ad."

"Oh, come off it, Zora, you don't fool me a bit. You've been dying to go to Pedersen about Paul for days. I wouldn't mind so much if you hadn't said you wouldn't, but—"

Zora laid both hands flat on the table. "Eileen, for Christ's sake, slow down and listen. I did not speak to Pedersen about it until today, when he asked me about the ad. Then all I did was say yes. That's all."

Eileen's eyes widened. "Are you telling me the truth? You didn't go to Pedersen? Well, who did? I didn't tell him."

They sat staring at each other.

"Would *Happy Times* have—no, the police wouldn't have known to ask," Eileen said.

"Didn't Pedersen talk to you, too?"

"Yes, he did—just a little while ago. He seemed to know everything. I was so busy being furious with you, I didn't pay much attention to what he said. I did ask who told him, but you know him—he never answers. He just asks another question."

"Well, there we are. I suppose there are a dozen ways he could have got hold of Paul's name. Probably Paul told him how we met."

"He must have. God, I hope Paul doesn't think this was my doing." Eileen picked up her soup spoon, looked into her bowl without appetite and laid the spoon down again.

"Relax—he'll know better. I wonder, though, what

that detective thinks. Do you suppose he thinks Paul killed Sally? Maybe he thinks Paul's out to get all of us."

"That's crazy. You do say the strangest things, Zora."

"I know. I'm becoming paranoid." Zora lit a cigarette.

"But why? Are you afraid of Paul?"

Zora shook her head uncertainly. "I'm afraid—in general, mostly." She smiled faintly. "It's most uncharacteristic of me."

"That's crazy. *I'm* not afraid of him."

"You're right. I am paranoid."

"I don't know, maybe you see—saw something in Paul that I . . ."

"I'm paranoid. That's it."

"You are. Anyway, you're wrong." She looked at her soup with distaste and picked up her spoon again. "Put that cigarette out, will you? I can't eat wrapped in smoke."

Zora crushed it out and picked up her own spoon. "Let's just stop." She smiled. "Let's eat lunch and not talk about it anymore. I was wrong."

"You were. We're just lucky it was he who answered our ad. You know, Zora, I think maybe you're jealous of Paul and me. You don't want me to get any sort of permanent—well, more or less permanent—relationship out of it. Are you wishing it were you he was interested in?"

Zora laughed. "No." She put down her spoon and reached across the table to squeeze Eileen's hand. "Believe me, it isn't that at all. I'll stop. Let's just not talk about it for now." She went back to her lunch.

Eileen was still a little stiff with her as they paused outside the restaurant to cross the street, Zora on her way down the mall to her shop, Eileen back to her car.

"Look, Eileen, I"—Zora was saying as they stepped off the curb—"*Watch out!*" A car veered suddenly and continued down the street.

Eileen gasped. "He nearly hit us!" She turned to Zora.

145

"You're as white as— Are you all right?" Zora's face was drained of color, shocked. "You saw who it was."

Zora took a deep breath. "No. No. I'm all right. I didn't see. It was just a blue car. We weren't looking where we were going."

"A blue car." Eileen's voice was flat. "Paul has a blue car."

CHAPTER TWENTY-ONE

Her front door stuck. For one hysterical moment, Eileen thought, like Sally's—my God, history repeating itself? Then the door gave.

Inside, the house seemed stuffy. She opened a window at each end of the living room and stood in the draft she had created, shivering slightly. The near accident had unstrung her. Although in the confusion of the moment she had barely seen the rear of the car far down the street, an image had formed itself of Paul's blue Toyota. It had been he. But why? Why should he try to run them down?

His phone number at the lab was in her address book;

147

she had never memorized it. It took two tries for her fingers to find the right buttons.

"Good afternoon. Richards Laboratories." The voice was uninterested, anonymous.

Eileen cleared her throat. "Is Dr. Shapiro in, please?"

"One moment. I'll ring."

She could hear the extension being rung, buzz after buzz. After a while, the voice returned. "I'm sorry, he must not have come in from lunch. May I take a message?"

"No. Yes. No, I'll call back." She put down the receiver with a trembling hand.

It needn't mean anything. The man had to eat lunch. And certainly if he were planning to run her down, he would hardly choose the mall in view of all the—alone in the silent room, she began to laugh, hearing the hysteria in her voice—in view of all the street people. When she was quiet, she scrubbed at her wet cheeks.

She was sure Paul was no murderer, but of what else was she sure? Only what he had told her, and it appeared he had not told her much. Only under pressure—she couldn't recall clearly, but she was sure she had pressed him—had he admitted to having seen Zora, and he had never mentioned Sally. But wasn't it Sally he had always been interested in when she had spoken of the three of them?

Once, early, she had asked Paul if he found Sally attractive, and he had said something noncommittal. Later, she remembered, she had said, "Do you ever run into her? Around town?" She knew she had suspected even then, been afraid to ask more. If he had nothing to conceal, if Sally had been unimportant to him, why had he lied? It was as she had feared—not feared, been sure, all along. He had been having an affair with Sally during the whole time she had known him.

And what of Zora? Was she keeping silent about some-

148

thing that had happened during that single time she had seen Paul? If it was a single time. They had both said it was just the once, and clearly Zora was more afraid than interested where Paul was concerned. If he and Zora had just talked, would he have told Zora something he hadn't told her? Not, she reflected with bitterness, that he seemed inclined to tell her anything.

She was being hysterical. But he had driven straight at them. Not going to the police about it was foolhardy. What was Paul to her, anyway? Only three months before she had never heard of him. She had a moment of longing for that past time. What did you do with people who came into your life when you were better off without them? Could you pretend you had never met? Each relationship with another human being, no matter how brief or glancing, in some subtle way changed you. My life wasn't idyllic, but I was contented then, before Paul, she thought; I wasn't riddled with anxiety like this.

A board creaked and she jumped. She rose and closed the windows. The house felt cold.

She could call Detective Pedersen and tell him about the car; it was crazy not to.

Another board creaked. She started nervously. Damn these old houses, she thought, why do I live in one?

She had made her decision. She would call Pedersen. As she reached for the phone, her doorbell rang. She put down the receiver.

CHAPTER TWENTY-TWO

On the first ring the door opened, as though she had been standing inside, waiting. There was a moment of silence before she spoke.

"*Your* blue car," she said. "You almost ran over us."

He stood, still outside the door she had opened, staring at her as though he were seeing her for the first time. "I didn't mean to, for God's sake. I was startled. Can I come in?"

Almost reluctantly, she stood back to let him enter.

"You nearly ran over us. Over me—that was it, wasn't it? Why?"

He looked around the room, dim in the sloping rays of afternoon sun that filtered through the blinds. "You know, you do have good taste," he said. "Did I ever tell you you had good taste?"

She gave a little grunt of denial or anger.

"All right. I nearly ran over you. Don't say it again. I just didn't expect to see you suddenly walk out in front of me that way."

"That was cause—"

He broke in impatiently. "You want me to go?" He turned, then reconsidered, took a chair and leaned back. "Sit down, for Christ's sake. Let's talk like a couple of civilized people."

Awkwardly, she perched on the outer rim of the chair opposite him.

"Sit back—relax. The world isn't about to come to an end. Listen, tell me what this is all about. I'm really in the dark. It's all been going too fast for me. I talked with that detective—did you know? I suppose you couldn't."

"It's about someone's death—Sally's death. Murder."

"I know that, but what's your connection with it?"

"You should know. From what I've been led to gather, you were in close communication with her."

"Close communication." He snorted. "What's going on?"

"You gave her my fetish."

"Well, that certainly can't be what it's all about. You were angry with me and gave it back. Was I supposed to put it in a safe, hold it sacred until you changed your mind? People who enjoy things should have them and use them. Isn't that what you always liked so much about my place?"

"The fetish was mine."

151

"It was yours because you admired it and wanted it. You returned it. She saw it and admired it. Actually, originally, if you recall, it was mine."

"Nothing matters to you, does it? You present yourself as this generous, sensitive man and then—"

"Break your heart? Is your heart broken?"

"Don't ridicule me. You know what I'm talking about."

"You don't go killing people over things like that." He stopped. After a moment, he touched her face. "I don't know why I said that. But you *did,* didn't you? I just this moment realized."

She buried her face in her hands. "I never meant to. I didn't—I never—it just happened. I looked down and saw it and picked it up—she was standing with her back to me. I didn't even know I had done it, till afterwards."

"It was me you really wanted to kill."

"No. It was Sally. No, that's not right—I didn't want to *kill* her. But it was the way she was, so smug. Everybody—all the men liked her, wanted her. I could never see why. She didn't really care—nothing mattered to her. She just tossed people aside. How could she—she wasn't that pretty, she wasn't that bright. She could act a little, maybe that was it. Did she play her part well with you?"

"Look." He leaned toward her, his voice gentle. "It wasn't anything she did or you did. These things happen. Chemistry, I guess. People react to each other—who knows why? We did—you and I. Sally and I did, in a different way. I've never compared you. You were different women."

"But after all those things you said—"

"People say things. They mean them when they say them. I meant—"

Before the sentence was out, with a suddenness that startled them both, there was a knock at the door, then a long ring of the doorbell.

"Who—?" She rose.

"Well, answer it."

She stood, examining his face. "Are you going to—?"

The bell rang again.

"For God's sake, answer it."

Slowly, she moved to the door, turned the knob, opened it.

Pedersen stood on the doorstep. "Mrs. Hirsch." He stepped inside. "And Mr. Carr. I thought I'd find you here, sir."

CHAPTER TWENTY-THREE

Afterwards, driving Freda back from the airport along the shadowed, winding highway, speaking into the dark of the car, Pedersen told her about it. "Funny," he said, "she looked so different when they brought her in. Her face had relaxed and she looked soft and pretty. And, you know," he added, "she didn't smoke at all."

"I'm glad," Zora said, as she faced Pedersen. "I was afraid." She did not elaborate. "I don't want a lawyer till

I've talked to you. I want you to understand." She seemed unable to go on.

Pedersen broke the silence. "What do you mean, you were afraid?"

She took a deep breath and began to speak slowly. "It wasn't you I was afraid of, that's not it. Let me tell you. It started the night we wrote the ad. Eileen's told you about the ad?"

"Dr. Shapiro told me."

"If he hadn't, I'd have told you. I had decided to tell you about Paul Shapiro, to do everything I could to make you suspect him. But I couldn't have lived with myself if I had succeeded." Her gaze at him was level. "I haven't much—I'm not easy with people the way Sally was, and I've never had what anyone else would consider a good relationship with a man. I don't even have any particular talents—oh, a good eye, but no talents. But I've always had principles, and I've lived by them. My father taught me the importance of integrity—it's the best thing I got from him. Maybe the only thing. I know now, absolutely, that I couldn't have lived with myself. But—I was afraid." She lowered her eyes. "Afraid I would."

Freda stirred. "Is it principled to kill someone?"

A dry sound came from Pedersen's throat. "Principle had nothing to do with the murder. The killing was something she never intended, a moment of fury, of . . . terribly wounded vanity, I suppose. I think self-hate is at the root of killings like that. But she recognized the difference between that and a calculatedly immoral act."

"It just seems like an odd notion of . . . priorities."

"Priorities have nothing to do with it, either, Freda." His voice was stern.

"All right." She sighed. "You probably understand it.

You know, you should have gone into psychology, I've always said so."

He laughed. "You have."

"Go ahead. What did she say next?"

"It began," Zora went on, "the night we wrote that ad. I didn't know Sally or Eileen well, and I had . . . defended myself against strong feelings after my breakup with Jim—sometimes it seemed as though I'd protected myself against feeling anything. You see, my marriage had never been any good. Andrew, my husband, was twenty years older than I. I was working on a doctorate and he was my chairman. I liked him; as for him, I was probably his mid-life fling."

A harsh sound caught in her throat. "Funny to think of him that way. Or me. Funnier. At any rate, he was what people call"—her face was wry—"a late bloomer. He'd never married." She looked at Pedersen with sadness. "He was witty, older, wise—like my father. I think I married him for that. But he was not any more sociable than I. We never had many friends together—couples. I had friends. He had a few. And the rest of it was over very quickly. He was past wanting children and terribly wrapped up in his work, and our life became—well, it was like what my friends who were having children called parallel play. We were together, but we were not engaged with one another. I did travel with him, and I developed an interest in rugs through that, but otherwise, nothing." She snapped her fingers. "Nothing.

"Then I had some trouble with a client who had bought some expensive rugs and, when it came time to pay the bill, questioned their value, and I called on Jim. I'd heard of him—he was with a big Chicago art auction house." She sat silent, remembering.

"I went to his office." Her face softened. "I had never seen anyone so . . . beautiful. I loved just to look at him.

I was never sure what he saw in me, but I adored him. Maybe"—she smiled without humor—"*that* was what he saw in me. Anyway. We met for lunch. Then dinner. Andrew never noticed my absence, nor my presence for that matter. Pretty soon Jim and I were spending every free moment together. It went on for over two years, the happiest two years of my life. Then suddenly, out of the blue, he announced that he had met someone else and was going to be married."

She smiled faintly. "I suppose, really, the wonder is that I didn't hit *him* with that fetish. Instead, I gave it back, along with everything else that he had given me."

"He was another piece of art to her, don't you suppose?" Freda said. "Like a beautiful Persian rug."

"Maybe originally. There was more to it than that." Far in the distance he could see the lights of the town. "I think it was that she'd never loved anybody since her father—not her mother, her husband, no one. She'd stored up all that feeling."

"Later, after my husband's death, I came to Bay Cove and met Sally and Eileen. I barely knew them, only in the most casual way, until the evening of the ad writing when we began to talk about ourselves. And then, as Sally talked, I learned I had become a friend of Jim's wife—former wife, by then, the woman who had turned my life upside down. It was just too much. It had been eight years, I was still mourning him, and here she was."

She stopped and then went on. "When she told us about him, I had a moment right then when I could have killed her. I had never felt such rage in my life—it washed over me like a tidal wave. Just for a moment. Then it passed. I never felt it again—even later when I hit her." She tilted her head back and looked directly into Pedersen's face. "A sad little tale, isn't it? Pathetic."

157

She went on. "I treated her like anyone else. I kept telling myself it didn't matter, it was long over, but there was something about the way Sally flaunted herself, the way she treated men as if none of them mattered, the way she talked about Jim—with contempt. It was hard not to feel resentful. I tried. I really thought I had it under control. I met her for lunches. We talked about the theater and rugs and things of no consequence. I even missed our threesomes—we weren't getting together any longer, the three of us."

She drew a deep breath. "Then Sunday evening, for no reason at all, I thought I'd drop by. I thought maybe I could tell her, we could talk about it—that that would help, would lay it to rest. I could never have let her laugh at me, but I thought I could tell it so she wouldn't. After all, he was out of her life now, too."

She sat forward in the chair. "And then—it all happened so fast it's hard to remember. She was poking at the fire, and I was standing by the coffee table. I looked down. There was my fetish figure. I had never before seen it in her house. And before I could take that in, I heard her saying over her shoulder, in that offhand way she had, 'I'm taking Jim Carr back—remember, my last husband? Number three? I suppose I shouldn't, but he's only in the country now and then, and it'll be nice to have a man around occasionally.' She was just about to turn—from her voice, I could hear she was smiling, maybe she was even going to say something about our ad—when I picked up the fetish. Afterwards, I couldn't believe I'd done it. I couldn't believe she wouldn't get up and say, 'What are you doing, Zora? That hurt.'"

"She never planned it," Freda said.
"No, we were sure from the beginning that it was unpremeditated."

158

"It's terrible," Freda said. "Terrible. For both of them."

"Murder is terrible."

"But—they were people like us. I'd met Sally Robinson. She was taking the part in the new play that I'd have tried out for if I hadn't been going to Carey's."

"I know."

"What did she say then?"

Zora covered her face. "It was awful. I never meant to kill her." After a while she spoke again. "I had just enough presence to let myself out. That damned door stuck, and I kept thinking I'd be trapped there—with her. While I was tugging at the door, I thought once of taking something so it would look like a burglary. I had wiped the fetish on my slip, I don't know why. But I couldn't go back." She shivered.

"After I got away, all I wanted to do was hide. I walked into a movie house and sat there, but I don't think I saw anything. Later I realized it was a film I'd seen years ago, *Lolita*. After a while I got up and walked out. I didn't look at a paper or listen to a news broadcast for two days; I just got in my car and kept moving. I kept thinking if I ignored it, it would just go away, be a bad dream. It was actually a shock when I heard she was dead. All I've thought since then was . . . not so much how to save myself as how to keep anyone from knowing."

Shame, Pedersen thought. It was that awful sense of shame that kept her silent.

"Then today," she went on, "when I saw Jim in that car, it was like . . . the dam breaking, I guess. I've kept my feelings under control for so long, it was a relief even to feel pain again. It was awful, but in some way it was wonderful. But too late. What will I do with my feelings

159

now?" She stopped and an odd expression came over her face. "I just remembered," she said.

"Remembered?"

"What my high school yearbook said. *Watch it with this one. Our Zora has a one-track mind.*" She laughed, a sharp, bitter sound. "They had my number. Now," she said, "I'll phone my lawyer."

"How did you know? When you went to Zora Hirsch's house?"

"It was a phone call. Jim Carr called to tell me he had been mistaken about a time he gave me. He said he had been shaken by Sally's death and hadn't been thinking straight. Then he added something. He said, 'As a matter of fact, I'm pretty shaken right now. This noon when I was on the mall in my rented Hertz, a woman I hadn't seen in years almost walked in front of the car. I'd known her pretty well and here I damned near ran over her.' Something just clicked with me. I said, 'A woman from Chicago?' and he said, 'Yes,' in a puzzled voice, as though he wasn't sure he hadn't told me that himself. I said, 'Tell me her name,' and he told me. He said, 'Her name was Zora Hirsch. I'm sure you've never heard of her.'"

"And things fell into place. You realized it wasn't Shapiro that Sally and her murderer had struggled over. It was Carr."

"Yes. It was that link—that relationship I couldn't have known about. But I did know Carr didn't just know women well. He went to bed with them."

"Did you guess about the fetish?"

"I realized it must have been part of it—a symbol in some sense."

"Sally had it stored away and took it out that Saturday because he was coming to the house?"

"Or because they were resuming their relationship."

"So that's it." After a moment she said, "That woman will go to prison?"

"What happens to her isn't up to us. The courts will take over now."

"But what do you think?"

They entered a short bright stretch, the street lamps of the town illuminating their faces. He turned to look at her in the light, small and neat, her dark head tilted toward him. "I think," said Pedersen, with feeling, "that it's about time you came home."

CHAPTER TWENTY-FOUR

"Will she get off?" Eileen had uneasily avoided the subject all evening, but she could no longer resist asking. "I mean, do you think she will?"

"It wasn't planned."

"Does that make it manslaughter?"

"Voluntary manslaughter, I think it's called."

"Anyway, not first degree. Is first degree the same as Murder One?"

"You've been watching television."

Eileen sighed. "I keep wondering which of us suggested that dumb ad in the first place. I hope it wasn't me. If we'd never had that first conversation . . . Not," she added, "that everything that came out of it was bad. Did you really tell Sally you wouldn't see her anymore?"

"I said I did."

"And . . ."

"I did not sleep with her."

"You were faithful to me." She smiled. "But you told me you wanted no commitments. Remember?"

They were on the rug before his fireplace. Over the weekend the weather had turned damp and cold; it was already a week into November. Eileen was wrapped in an old frayed sweater of Paul's, hand-knit for him by someone. Perhaps his wife. She had not asked.

"I know I said that. I hate to be pushed."

"Pushed?"

"That's right."

"I was pushing?" They were quiet for a while; then she said, "Paul, we've never talked about it. Why didn't you tell me the truth? Why did you lie?"

"I didn't precisely lie. Though"—his laugh was bitter—"my wife used to say I preferred lying to telling the truth. It was a challenge to my creativity."

"Is that true?"

"In some ways, I think it is."

"Won't I ever be able to trust you?"

"I don't know what you'll be able to do. Since we're asking hard questions, will I be able to trust you? Why did you go to the police about me?"

She laughed shortly. "We've certainly talked about that. I told you I didn't. You'll never believe me. I almost did call them though, when I thought you were trying to run us over. I was afraid. Zora was—said she was afraid. I suddenly felt I didn't know you. I had my hand right on the phone to call when a girl selling Girl Scout cookies rang my doorbell."

"I should send a check to the Girl Scouts. Do you feel you know me now?"

"I'm not sure either of us really knows the other. I do know I love you."

He swung around to look into her face. "I've gotten used to you, too." He smiled. "Would you call that love?"

"I wait all day . . ."

"I do, too."

He pulled her to him. "I do lie. Not always, but sometimes. I'm far from perfect—just ask my ex-wife."

"I guess I am, too." Her voice was small. "I didn't show much trust, when it came right down to it. I was more worried about my neck than . . ."

"Than mine?"

"Almost. Wouldn't it have been awful if . . ." She shivered.

"If what? I've been noticing. You don't finish sentences."

Eileen sighed and then giggled. "And I've been lying here thinking you still haven't gotten around to repairing that drafty window."

He rolled to his side, facing her. "Know something? We sound married. I guess the next step . . ." He stopped. Then he said, "God. Now I'm doing it."

She laughed. "I guess so," she said. "I guess that is the next step."